GW00400235

THE PRINCESS'S BODYGUARD

EMILY HAYES

1

TABITHA

Princess Tabitha was sure she'd made it. She glanced nervously over her shoulder, but she didn't see anyone. Of course, that didn't mean much. They could turn up at a moment's notice, swarming around her like locusts. The press were like that.

Most of Tabitha's family had gotten used to it— it was part of being British Royalty, after all—but Tabitha still hated it. That was why she'd declined doing her shopping in London. She had traveled all the way to Bakewell, where she was sure no one would find her.

It was a small town, but there was a market here, and she longed to do some clothes shopping that wasn't online only. There would be more choice online, but Tabitha loved being able to try on clothes and look at them in person without being harassed by reporters.

She got off the bus and walked into town, pulling her shawl closer around her head. She knew how recognisable she was so she was wearing clothes she definitely wouldn't normally wear and sunglasses and a shawl over her hair and had her security team well briefed to stay at a distance and try to blend in. As the queen's daughter, her face was well-known throughout the whole of the UK.

At first, the excursion went well. Tabitha wandered between stands, picking up things and buying here and there. She was careful not to flash too much money around, not wanting to draw attention to herself.

She was just buying a new dress when it all went wrong.

"Hey! Are you—are you Princess Tabitha?"

Tabitha felt her face going red. She wasn't going to lie, but the last thing she wanted was to cause a scene. "Excuse me," she murmured, trying to slip past him.

"You are! Lizzy, look, it's Princess Tabitha!"

His shout drew a small crowd at once. Tabitha

did her best not to grimace. She knew it wouldn't be polite to flee from people who were only excited to see her, so she did her best to smile and greet each one of them.

Of course, that wasn't the end of it. It never was.

Even small towns like these had reporters, and commotions like this one drew reporters like moths to a flame.

"Princess Tabitha! Princess Tabitha! What made you decide to come to Bakewell?"

A camera and microphone were shoved in her face. Tabitha tried to turn away, but the reporter just moved with her, not allowing her to escape. Her security team moved in quickly and started moving people away from Tabitha.

"I just wanted to do some shopping in peace. Please, leave me be."

"Why did you come all the way out here? Is there friction between you and your family that sent you so far out?"

Tabitha resisted the urge to roll her eyes. They were always so insistent on creating conspiracy theories out of nothing. "My family and I are fine, thank you. Now please, move aside. I need to go."

She dodged the reporter and exited at a swift walk, ignoring the trail of people that followed her.

Tabitha bit back tears as she nodded to her head of security who was close by. She knew he would have the driver there straight away. Before Tabitha knew it, Jason was waiting for her with the limo and Tabitha gratefully stepped inside. By now, she had a small entourage of people trailing after her.

Why can't I just be free?

She hated it. She hated that this was her life. All she wanted was a break. If she could just take a brief holiday from all of this drama. She'd been dealing with it her whole life. If she could only have a small respite, she was sure that she'd be able to get back to handling it in her daily life.

The thought brought Tabitha up short.

Who's to say she couldn't have that? Why not go on holiday, somewhere far away where no one would recognize her?

She'd always wanted to visit the U.S. People there might know her name but probably not her face, not as well as the people of the UK at least. She just needed a better disguise. New hair and new style, she should be okay.

Tabitha brightened as the idea took hold.

She'd have to sell her mother on it, of course, but Mary wasn't unreasonable. She knew how much Tabitha had been struggling with all the constant attention from the public recently.

She got home and went straight to her mother's office.

"Hi, Mom."

"Hi, sweetie. How did your secret shopping go?"

"Not good," Tabitha sighed. "I'm going to have to do it online. I got accosted by press again."

Mary's expression softened in sympathy. "I'm sorry, Tabitha. I know you hate it, but it's just an unavoidable part of being who we are."

"I know. I can handle it... I just think I need a little break."

"You've tried that before. Staying shut up in the palace and not emerging may keep the press away, but it isn't good for your mental health."

"You're right—that's not what I mean. I was thinking more like a holiday."

"A holiday?"

"Yeah. What if I went to visit the U.S. like I always wanted to? I would be much less likely to be recognized there."

"That's true," Mary mused. "It could be dangerous, though. You'd have to take a large contingent of security."

"No, Mother," Tabitha groaned. "That would entirely defeat the point. If I have a swarm of British police around me, it'll be a dead giveaway."

"I'm not sending you to a foreign country with no one protecting you!"

Tabitha supposed she was right. Like it or not, there were threats associated with who she was. There were any number of people who would love to do her harm if they got the opportunity.

"What if we hired an American bodyguard? That way, they would blend in and wouldn't blow my cover."

"That's something I could consider. We'd still have to plan this carefully, though. A lot could go wrong."

Tabitha thought Mary was a little paranoid, but she didn't say so. Mary had been living in the role of royalty for a lot longer than she had, after all. "I'm happy to take safety measures. I don't want to be reckless. I just really need a break."

Mary's expression softened. "I know you do, honey. Dealing with the constant publicity can be wearying. We all need a break at some point. You should at least take Alice with you. I don't want you going without anyone from our household."

"That'll be fine. I'll be glad to have Alice with me."

Tabitha couldn't clean to save her life, and Alice the maid was a wizard with household chores.

"Excellent. Then I suppose we should start planning."

Tabitha felt excitement curling in her belly. Not only would she finally see America, but she would have a chance at escaping the constant scrutiny she was under. It was a dream come true. Having a bodyguard would be nothing new. She'd needed to give bodyguards the slip before, just like she did to go on her doomed shopping trip.

One way or another, she was going to enjoy her trip to the U.S. to the fullest.

2

JK

JK Sullivan got up and made her coffee. She ate breakfast and went to sit in the beautiful little garden outside her apartment. She stared off into the distance and... did nothing.

Fuck, she was bored. Retirement certainly wasn't all it was cracked up to be. She had thought that taking an early retirement from her successful military career would be idyllic, but it wasn't. It was just damn boring.

She needed something to do. After her disastrous attempts at hiking and attending a book club, she wasn't keen to try any more conventional hobbies. She needed something *exciting*. Something that had real stakes to it, like the life she was used to.

Bored out of her mind, JK started scrolling through her phone's contacts, wondering if she could call up anyone for coffee. Of course, most of her friends were busy at work at this time, so it was unlikely she'd find any solutions this way.

She stopped as she scrolled past one particular contact.

Gray was an old friend from her army days. They didn't speak often, but they had kept in touch. JK knew that Gray ran a successful body-guard business and she had taken on many ex-military members as part of her workforce.

Would she be interested in hiring JK? It would certainly be something to do, and there would be real stakes involved.

JK had never been one to sit around and go back and forth over a decision. She hesitated for only a moment before pressing the call button.

"Hello?"

"Oh—sorry, I might have the wrong number. Is Gray there?"

"Yes! This is her wife. I'll go get her. Gray, there's a call for you!"

A moment later, Gray's familiar voice came across the line. "Hello?"

"Hi, Gray. It's JK Sullivan."

"JK! How are you doing? How's retired life treating you?"

"Not that well," JK admitted. "I'm honestly bored out of my mind. I need something to do. I was wondering... Well, if you have any vacancies and you think I might work well for them..."

"I always have room for someone with your skillset. I've got a whole folder and videos on how to transition military skills into guarding civilians. I can send it over, if you'd like, and you can let me know if it's something you'd be interested in."

"That would be great, thank you."

"Excellent. Let me know if you'd like to go ahead and I'll send you a case. Business is booming and we have no shortage of them, so you'd be able to start pretty soon, I'm sure of that."

This was already sounding wonderful. JK thanked Gray again and hung up. She spent the next few hours reading through Gray's extensive files and watching the videos. It was a lot to take in, but the actual content of what she had to do didn't seem that difficult.

She had the hard skills she needed already.

Most of it was an interpretation of what seemed like frequently irrational and infuriating civilian behavior.

JK could do this. She was sure there would be some frustrations involved, but it would be worth it. Anything would be better than sitting here at home, slowly losing her mind.

She emailed Gray saying that she'd love the job. A mere hour later, she got a response with a folder on a potential new client. JK felt her eyebrows rising as she read. Princess Tabitha of the British Royal Family? Gray must trust her more than she had realized if she was assigning royalty to her on her very first case. Why would a British Princess be looking for an American bodyguard? Surely the British Royals looked after their own Princesses?

It seemed that Gray did thorough research on all of her clients before handing them over to individual employees, because she had a detailed docket on Princess Tabitha.

JK read through it carefully several times, knowing that Tabitha's life could very well depend on her thoroughness. It seemed that Tabitha was a simple, young naïve royal. Protecting her should be easy. She was young and just wanted to see some of the world. It wasn't like anyone was after her. She simply wanted an American bodyguard to help her blend in better during her time here and she planned to be living undercover anyway.

She sent a response to Gray, saying she'd take the case. Tabitha was set to arrive two days from now. She would be staying in a mansion out in the countryside, and Gray would be staying there with her.

It sounded like a lot of fun—certainly more fun than sitting here alone at home.

JK spent the next two days doing some additional research on Tabitha. She was disappointed not to find much except press releases on her shopping trips. Many photos of Tabitha's long blonde hair beautifully done and her big green eyes engaging audiences. Tabitha seemed to hate publicity and actively stayed away from the media bar official royal engagements. JK would have preferred to have more information on her client, but she supposed that could wait until she could talk to the princess in person.

So, two days later, she packed a small bag of essentials and took the long taxi ride to the mansion that would be her home for the next few weeks.

3

TABITHA

Tabitha was practically vibrating with excitement. She was finally in America, and she intended to do everything she couldn't do in the U.K. Her hair had been cut into a trendy messy bob and dyed a rich chocolate brown. She had brown contact lenses to cover her own eye color. She had big sunglasses. She was dressing more casually than she ever had in public. She was confident she wasn't recognisable and really hoped for it to stay that way. She practically bounced up the steps to the house where she and Alice would be staying, only to be brought up short by the sight before her.

An extremely attractive woman with close cropped brown hair and an air of general toughness and competence was standing at the top of the stairs. Tabitha could just see streaks of gray at her temples, which made her look distinguished as well as hot. How old was she? Maybe mid 40s Tabitha thought to herself.

"Hi, Tabitha. I'm JK Sullivan. Ex US Army Captain. I'll be your bodyguard while you're here."

JK held out a hand for Tabitha to shake. Tabitha gulped. *This* was her bodyguard? Did they really have to assign her someone so attractive? Tabitha wasn't out at all, she was very very very much in the closet even though she had no doubt at all now at 28 years old that she was very much a lesbian.

Nobody in the British Royal Family had ever come out either privately or publicly that Tabitha knew of and she dreaded being the first. She had absolutely no intention of letting the world know she was gay until she was good and ready, if that day ever came. Why did this bodyguard have to be so hot and *gay* looking? Tabitha wanted her instantly, but she knew if she made a move on her new bodyguard it was bound to get back to her mother.

She held out a shaky hand, which JK took in a firm grip. "It's nice to meet you. I've already reviewed the security around the house and it's top-notch. You won't be in any danger while you're here. It's when you're out and about that we'll need to be vigilant, but you just leave that to me." JK gave her a kind smile, the corners of her eyes crinkling a little. "You just do what you came here to do—relax and have fun. I'll do all the hard work."

Tabitha liked JK already. "I'd like to go clubbing."

JK winced. "Okay."

"Okay, what? I saw that look."

"It's just that clubs are extremely insecure places. There are lots of opportunities to be attacked without your attacker ever risking themselves. However, no one knows you are here and there is no evidence of any threat to your life, so I don't see why you shouldn't be allowed to go clubbing. I'll just have to keep a close watch for any potential trouble."

Good, at least they were on the same page. "Then let's go out."

"Don't you want to unpack your things?"

"Alice can unpack for me. I want to stop by the mall anyway to see what American fashion is like in person; I've only seen it online. I can pick up something to wear at the club there—and something for you as well."

JK looked down at her practical brown pants and her short-sleeved button-up blouse. "What's wrong with this?"

Tabitha rolled her eyes. "That outfit screams *working professional*—which is great when meeting a new client for the first time, but not as much when you're out clubbing. Don't worry, we'll find something for you."

"I suppose," JK conceded.

Tabitha made sure Alice was okay to carry the bags before leading the way to the car. The driver they had hired for her time here was waiting for them.

"To the nearest mall, please."

"Of course, Princess."

"Please, call me Tab. I'm supposed to be flying under the radar."

"Yes, Princess."

Tabitha rolled her eyes again and turned to JK. "You're going to use my first name, right?"

"Absolutely. Your best safety is in anonymity. I'm not going to draw attention to who you are and potentially draw trouble in around us."

"Good." No one would hear Jack the driver

calling her Princess from inside the car, but if JK started using that word when they were out and about, it wouldn't take long for people to put two and two together.

Tabitha pulled her dark glasses down over her face and messed her hair up a bit more just to be sure. She liked this short hairstyle. It was so easy and felt so free, rather than her usual long immaculate blonde curls that had her spending hours in her hairdressers chair every few days.

They got to the mall and Tabitha stepped inside, taking a deep breath, relishing the freedom. Her heart was beating fast. There were people everywhere, but nobody was looking at her. Nobody was noticing her. Maybe she was anonymous for once. Here, she could browse shops to her heart's content without having to fear being accosted by reporters.

"Let's go this way!"

She headed to a sparkling store that had some designer dresses in the front window. Tabitha soon had a full cart of things to try on. She turned to JK. "Go on, pick something to wear. My treat."

"I'm really okay with what I'm wearing."

"They're not going to let you into the club like that. Live a little, JK, come on," she pleaded, giving her best puppy eyes, that she hoped even with the new contact lenses would have the desired effect.

JK's tough face softened and her brown eyes warmed to Tabitha and Tabitha felt a flood of desire run through her body.

"I suppose I do need to be admitted into the club with you," JK conceded. "I don't really know what counts as suitable club attire, though. Perhaps you could advise me?"

Tabitha got to choose what to dress JK in? Even better. "Of course! How about this?"

Tabitha pulled out a short, tight, red dress that would have looked spectacular on JK's athletic body but clearly would not be her style. JK gave it a doubtful look.

"I can't wear a dress! Look at me! I'm a masculine lesbian."

Tabitha felt thrills run through her when the word *lesbian* emerged from JK's lips. *Lesbian.*

Of course she is.

So am I.

But, nobody knows.

And I've never... you know... done it with a woman...

But I want to... more than anything else in the world.

"Right. Okay, how about this, then?" Tabitha took a deep breath and picked up some smart black dress pants and a sparkly gold shirt.

JK winced. "Does it have to be so... sparkly?"

"Sparkly is fun! You'll see, it'll be great."

"Um... I'm not sure its my color," JK muttered, but she took the outfit anyway.

A few minutes later, when JK came out of the changing room, Tabitha immediately regretted her choice of outfits for JK. She had thought it would make JK look hot, and dear God, it did. Tabitha's mouth was practically watering. JK's six-pack was just visible where the shirt was cropped just above where the pants sat at her hips.

No, she reminded herself. *No making a move on your bodyguard. Not only can she kick your ass, but she can expose you. She's off-limits.*

"Well? Does this suffice?"

"It's perfect," Tabitha squeaked. She dashed into her own changing room, fanning her face, hoping that JK hadn't noticed her blush.

She wanted to make JK as flustered as she felt. Was JK into her? Or did JK just see her as a silly little rich girl?

She chose a purple satin top that was cut so low her breasts were in danger of falling out. She found a skirt in a matching purple that barely covered her ass. Tabitha had always wanted to wear something like this, but the rules on clothing were so strict when she was in the UK. There were so many stifling old fashioned rules to being a royal, Tabitha relished in the thought that she might get looked at when she was out, for her body rather than *who* she was.

When Tabitha danced out of the changing room in the skirt and top, her hopes were confirmed. JK's face went bright red as her eyes automatically dropped down to Tabitha's breasts. She quickly looked up and took a deep breath. "You look wonderful."

"Thanks." Tabitha spun around, letting the skirt flutter around her ass, showing a flash of pink panties. JK's gaze was heavy with desire as she looked at Tabitha, and Tabitha half-expected JK to kiss her, but JK took a step back and another deep breath. "If you're done here, we should go pay."

"I'm not done yet. I never get to try clothes on, at least not without getting accosted. I'm going to take full advantage of this. Anyway, I need some new outfits so I've got plenty of things that are as far away from my usual outfits as we can get."

JK obligingly pushed the cart with the increasingly huge pile of clothes that Tabitha had tried on. It was a big store and they had clothes for all occasions. Of course, Tabitha had plenty of clothes, but she loved shopping and wasn't going to turn down the opportunity to do so with no pressure on her to finish as fast as possible before the press turned up.

"You should get this, too."

JK raised an eyebrow at Tabitha. "Where would I ever wear an evening gown?"

"We're sure to go to some fancy events while I'm here, and you want to fit in, don't you?"

"I suppose... All this stuff is expensive, though. I could probably borrow something from a friend for an event like that."

"No way. We're getting you something to keep. Will you try it on?"

"Not a dress, Tab... please.. I did say."

"Masculine lesbian. Right. Okay, how about this?"

Tabitha picked out some dress pants, a silk shirt and a black blazer. They did look smart and Tabitha looked at JK hopefully.

JK nodded acceptance although didn't look as delighted as Tabitha had hoped.

Her dark eyes looked more complicated than

Tabitha had seen yet. There was so much about this woman that Tabitha wanted to know.

Tabitha chuckled at JK's weary acceptance. So far, JK had been very tolerant. It was clear that shopping for designer clothes wasn't exactly her idea of a fun time, much less when she was one of the subjects of said shopping, but she had been a good sport and didn't show any signs of impatience.

By the time they were done, Tabitha's stomach was grumbling. "Any ideas for where you want to go for lunch?"

"I don't typically frequent malls, I'm afraid, so your guess is as good as mine."

"I guess we'll just have to take a look."

Tabitha sighed happily as she and JK wandered through the mall, peering into the different stores and looking at all the available restaurants. Being able to do this without being harassed was bliss.

"How about here?" She pointed to a traditional American diner.

JK raised an eyebrow. "I would have thought you'd go for something fancier."

"Oh, we will go to fancy restaurants, but I also

want to get a feel for the local culture. That's part of the fun."

"Sure. Whatever you'd like."

Tabitha ordered a burger, fries, a milkshake and a piece of pie. "Fast metabolism," she explained to JK, who was looking at her piled plate in surprise. "I've always been able to eat what I want. It drives my friends mad."

"Yes, I can imagine it would do that." JK took a careful bite of her own burger, which she had ordered with a salad and a diet soda. "What's it like, trying to maintain friendships being who you are?"

"It's difficult," Tabitha admitted. "Most people who surround me are either after my fame or my money. It's been difficult weeding out people who really want me for me, and sometimes, I'm not even sure whether I've really done a good job of it. I love hanging out with my friends, but I often wonder if I wasn't who I am, would they really want to spend time with me?"

"That sounds really lonely."

"It is." Tabitha shrugged. "It's part of the life, though. I have a lot of things most people could only ever dream of."

"Yes, but human connection is a basic need,

just as much as all the things money can buy you are. It shouldn't be underestimated. I'm sorry you have to go through that."

"Thanks, JK. What about you? What made you get into this line of work?"

"Honestly? Retirement wasn't suiting me at all. I got bored. I needed something to do, and this seemed like a worthwhile thing."

"So, I'm your distraction?"

"Something like that."

"Well, I like distracting you." The words even surprised Tabitha as they came out of her mouth.

JK went red again and took a big bite of her burger. . Tabitha was curious at JK's reaction to her. She didn't get to interact with queer women usually. She couldn't exactly seek them out—that was a dead giveaway for herself.

"So, JK, how long have you known you liked women?"

JK choked violently on her bite of burger. Tabitha waited patiently for her to stop coughing.

"What kind of question is that?"

"I'm just curious. You don't have to answer if you don't want to."

"No, it's okay. I was just surprised. Most people don't ask those questions."

"I'm not most people. And... well, I saw how you looked at me in that skirt."

"I'm sorry. That was inappropriate."

"Don't be sorry. I liked it," Tabitha said shyly.

"Well, I'm glad my embarrassment serves some purpose, at least. As for knowing I'm gay, I figured it out pretty early on. I was never interested men. When I kissed a woman for the first time when I was 18, I realized why I wasn't into guys."

Tabitha wondered if she should come out to JK. She wanted to have fun while she was here, and she wouldn't say no to a fling or two. If JK was following her, she was bound to figure it out sooner or later. It was probably better to get ahead of things and just tell her now.

And yet, as logical as that was, when she opened her mouth, Tabitha's nerve deserted her. She had never come out to anyone before, not even her closest friends and family, and she barely knew JK. Still, she had to do something to ensure JK's silence.

"JK, are you in contact with my mother at all?"

"I am. Well, you're mother's office. Her people. They are the ones who hired me, after all."

It wasn't the answer Tabitha had been hoping to hear, and perhaps JK realized that.

"Is that a problem?"

"I just... I really wanted to use this time to let my hair down a little. Relax and have fun, you know? But if you're reporting back to her..."

"I am not reporting back to her!" JK took a breath and softened her indignant tone. "I would never do that to you, Tab. Your mom may be the one who hired me, but Queen of England or not, you are still my client, and you deserve your privacy. Unless you pose a danger to yourself or others, I have no reason to tell anyone what you get up to, and that includes your mother. All I meant is that we've been in contact to exchange practical details, though most of that goes through Gray, my boss."

"Are you sure, JK? There are things about me... Well, I have secrets. Nothing dangerous, but certainly stuff that I don't want anyone finding out about."

"Your secrets are safe with me," JK said steadily. "Honestly, I don't even follow British politics. I'm not interested in whatever drama you could get involved in back home."

When Tabitha came out—*if* she came out—it would be a worldwide sensation. It would reach the ears of even those who didn't generally follow the royal family.

She looked into JK's eyes but saw no hint of dishonesty there. Maybe she was naïve to trust her after only just meeting her, but Tabitha didn't think that JK would sell her out.

"Great. Then let's go clubbing!"

Tabitha paid the bill and led the way back to the car. JK stuck close by her side, looking in all directions as they walked.

"Come on, let's get changed in the bathroom. We can't walk into the club like this."

JK sighed but didn't protest as she followed Tabitha to the bathroom. She checked the stall before allowing Tabitha in and took a stall of her own, eyeing her outfit gloomily as Tabitha handed it to her.

When Tabitha came out, JK was already changed, and if she'd thought having seen her once would reduce the wave of molten desire that went through her when she saw JK, she had been dead wrong.

JK looked like a sex goddess come to walk Earth. Tabitha wanted nothing more than to kiss her. she imagined JK pulling her skirt and panties off and going down on her right here on the bath-room counter.

"Tabitha? Are you alright?"

"Yes! Of course," Tabitha squeaked. "Shall we go?" She didn't think that JK would be impressed should Tabitha kiss her. JK had been kind to her, but she was also clearly serious about her job and Tabitha didn't think she would tolerate any such distractions. That didn't stop Tabitha from fanta-sizing, though.

They got back to the car and Tabitha climbed in, closely followed by JK.

"Right, Jack, to the nearest club, please."

"Of course, Princess."

Tabitha rolled her eyes.

They were just turning down a long, winding road that led to what was obviously a club when JK shook her head. "Oh, no. We are so not going in there. I can tell just from here that that place is shady as hell."

"I want to go clubbing," Tabitha protested. "You said I could." She tried not to sound sulky, but it was difficult, given how much she was looking forward to this.

"You can still go clubbing, but not here. Let's pick somewhere else, okay?"

"Where do you recommend?"

"I'm not exactly familiar with the local club-bing scene." JK sighed in frustration. "Jack, do you know of any clubs that are classy please?"

"Of course. I'll take you up Twelfth Avenue—there are a number of exclusive clubs there."

"Perfect." Tabitha settled back in her seat, shooting sidelong glances at JK. JK's gaze was flit-ting between the viewpoints of the different windows, ever watchful.

Tabitha wished JK would watch her the way she was watching JK, but JK was too busy doing her job well to be openly lusting after Tabitha.

They arrived at another club. Tabitha person-ally couldn't tell what made this one less shady than the other, but JK seemed satisfied, so they got out and went to the small line at the entrance. The bouncer let them through with no trouble, and then they were inside.

Tabitha had only been to clubs in London a few times before. She had been mobbed by people and had not enjoyed the experience. Now, she felt totally anonymous and was so hopeful for more from this night.

Tabitha hesitated for a moment, wondering whether she wanted to dance or get a drink. She glanced at JK, who looked incredibly uncomfortable, probably both because of her surroundings and what Tabitha had her wearing. The poor woman could probably use a drink.

Tabitha led the way to the bar and ordered something sparkly and fizzy from the menu.

"Just a water for me, please."

"Come on, JK, have a drink with me!"

"I can't drink, Tab—I'm working."

Oh. She supposed she should have thought of that. JK couldn't do her job if she was under the influence.

Tabitha drained the rest of her drink. "Then come dance with me!"

JK nodded and stood up, following Tabitha out onto the dance floor. It was a mark of how successful the club was that it was packed at this time. Tabitha didn't know much about clubs, but she knew that late late was generally their busiest period.

The music was upbeat and fun, and Tabitha immediately started dancing. She expected JK's dance moves to be stiff and unnatural, given that JK was clearly uncomfortable with the whole club scene, but JK surprised her, dancing like she was born for it.

If she kept watching JK moving to the music, Tabitha knew she was going to lose control entirely and kiss her, so she deliberately looked away.

One woman in particular caught her eye. She was young and stunning, almost as attractive as JK. Tabitha danced her way over and the woman easily fell in behind her.

"I'm Rose," she purred in Tabitha's ear.

"Tabitha." Tabitha grinned as Rose's hands came to rest on her hips, the two of them swaying to the music.

Rose felt delectable against her, and Tabitha closed her eyes, imaging that it was JK.

Rose spun Tabitha around and the next thing Tabitha knew, she was being kissed for the very first time.

She was so surprised that her mouth fell open, and Rose took immediate advantage of it. Her tongue slithered into Tabitha's mouth, and the feeling was so divine that Tabitha moaned and wrapped her arms around Rose's neck, pulling her in closer.

The next thing she knew, she and Rose were being wrenched apart by an irate JK.

"Get out of here," JK snapped at Rose.

"JK! What the hell?"

"Do you know what she is, Tab?"

"Should I?"

"Were you planning on paying for her time?"

Oh. *Oh.* Tabitha looked at Rose, who didn't appear remotely abashed. "Just trying to make a living...girrrl... chill out..."

Tabitha felt tears threatening to spring forth. It had been her first kiss ever, and it had been a lie. She didn't have any problem with sex workers, but she wanted her first time to be with someone who wanted her for her, not for her money.

Now, her first kiss could never be that.

She was just glad that JK had stopped her before it had gone any further.

"Tab? Are you alright?"

"I think I want to go home," Tabitha whispered. She didn't know if JK could hear her over the music or not, but she made a beeline for the door, and JK followed without question.

Tabitha bolted into the car. "Take us home, Jack," she mumbled. JK got in after her and the car started moving. She turned away from JK, trying to hide her tears.

"I'm sorry I upset you, Tabitha. I just didn't think you should be getting involved with an escort without knowing what you were getting into. If you want to go back and pay for her services, we can do that."

"No, it's not that. It's just... That was my first kiss."

"Oh, Tab, I'm sorry. I don't imagine that was what you wanted for your first kiss."

Tabitha shook her head, tears spilling down her cheeks. JK probably thought she was silly. Just some stupid royal who had nothing more to worry about than who she chose to kiss. Tabitha knew that JK was ex-military and had probably seen more than Tabitha could imagine.

The next thing she knew, JK's arms were around her. Tabitha buried her head in JK's shoulder as she cried, wishing more than anything that she could take the stupid club trip back, but it was too late for that.

"Tab, I know that first kisses are important, and you can't ever get that back, but I promise, there will be many more kisses in your future. When you find the right person, it won't matter that they're not the first person you kissed. It'll only matter that they're the last."

She was right. Of course she was right. Tabitha took several shaky breaths. She was feeling a little better now, but it felt so good to be in JK's arms that she didn't want to leave quite yet.

She finally had to when the car came to a stop at their country house.

"Can you walk?" JK asked quietly.

As much as Tabitha liked the idea of JK carrying her inside, she decided that this would be pushing it, given that she could definitely walk.

"Yes, I'm okay." She wiped her eyes on her sleeve. "Thanks, JK. You've done more than you needed to as my bodyguard."

"I may be your bodyguard, but I'm not a heartless robot. I'm not just going to see you in pain and not do anything about it."

Tabitha chuckled. "The british police I'm used to pretty much are heartless robots—at least, when it comes to me. I mean, I know they're not bad people and they obviously have people they care about, but to them, I'm just a job. A very important job. They don't care if I'm upset, as long as I'm safe."

"Well, I care. And you don't need to worry about me telling anyone about your secret." JK helped Tabitha out of the car and closed the door for her. "If you are into women, that is none of anyone else's business unless you choose to make it their business. No one will be hearing about your sexuality from me, I guarantee you that."

"Thank you, JK." Though she had been sure before now that JK wouldn't betray her to her mother, it was still nice to hear the assurance. "I think I just want to go to bed."

"I'll check the room for you."

Tabitha let JK clear the room before falling into bed. She did her best to put the experience in the club behind her and move on. She had always tried to look at things positively, or if there wasn't a positive way to look at them, simply focus on what positives were to be had.

Her first real clubbing experience had been an epic failure, but she still had JK as a bodyguard. JK was kind and devoted... not to mention hot.

Maybe... Maybe JK could be everything Tabitha wanted.

JK had had plenty of opportunities to make a move on her and she hadn't, but that was probably because she was trying to be professional. Tabitha knew that JK was attracted to her. All she needed to do was show JK that she needn't be all that professional.

Perhaps this could be the start of something truly wonderful.

4

JK

J K woke up early to check on the security cameras, but everything was calm. She showered and got dressed but didn't eat yet. She wanted to share breakfast with Tabitha when she woke up.

In the three hours it took Tabitha to wake up, JK chose to remain outdoors where she enjoyed the early sunshine whilst patrolling the perimeter of the property and familiarising herself with it and where all the cameras were and checked that all the locks on the doors and windows were working correctly. Everything was exactly as it should be.

When Tabitha woke up, she wandered through to the dining room, her hair adorably mussed. JK followed her and was surprised to see that the table was already stacked with food.

"Um... how did all this get here?"

"Dan, I imagine."

"Dan?"

"I can't cook to save my life, so we have Dan for that. I'm sure you can say hello to him if you like."

JK poked her head into the kitchen and sure enough, there was a man in a chef's uniform working at the stove.

"JK, right? Bacon is nearly ready. If you'd like to take a seat, I'll have it out to you in no time."

"How did you know when to get the food ready?"

"Tabitha's chef in the U.K. got hold of me. He let me know what Tabitha's patterns and preferences are so that I can get food ready for her in good time."

JK was curious as to what secrets Dan knew, but her stomach chose that moment to grumble loudly. She chuckled. "I guess I'll go join Tabitha for breakfast, then. Thanks, Dan."

Tabitha was already tucking into a bowl of fruit salad. JK sat down next to her, helping herself to fruit salad as well.

"How did you sleep?"

Tabitha shrugged. "Not the best. First night away from home and all that. You?"

"Perfectly. I've had to learn to get what sleep I can, when I can. As long as there is no one shooting at me, I sleep like a baby."

"That's a pretty low bar."

"Over here it is."

"You must have seen some pretty hectic stuff."

"Yeah. I didn't have it as bad as some, though. All in all, I got off fairly easily."

"What's the scariest thing that happened to you over there?"

It wasn't a pleasant thought, but JK reminded herself that Tabitha was just innocently curious and not trying to stir up bad memories. "I suppose the scariest was when a member of my unit was taken captive. We managed to get him back, mostly unharmed, but those three days were the longest of my life."

"You must have really cared about him."

"I did. My unit was like my family over there. I'd have done anything for them."

"You care. I like that about you. I like *you*, JK."

JK caught Tabitha's big green eyes looking fixing her own. She was beautifully natural this morning.

No contact lenses, her own eyes were enchanting. Her brown bob was messier than yesterday and her legs were long and tan in little PJ shorts and a cropped top.

Fuck, she is so beautiful.

"Thank you. I like you as well, Tabitha." Tabitha was sweet and naïve and very sheltered, but JK didn't hold that against her. She'd led a very sheltered life. JK was doing her best not to blush, but she feared she was failing miserably.

What was it about Tabitha that made her feel like a schoolgirl all over again?

Tabitha let her hand slide under the table to rest on JK's thigh. JK stiffened. Was Tabitha trying to kill her? Make her expire where she sat from sheer unrealized desire? Because if she was, she was doing a pretty good job at it.

"Tabitha, that's not a good idea."

Tabitha was nearly twenty years younger than her. Aside from who she was, JK definitely didn't date women in their 20s.

"Why not?" Tabitha asked innocently, her green eyes sparkling as she slid her hand further up JK's thigh. JK gently took her hand and removed it, placing it firmly on the table.

"We're from completely different worlds. I'm *so*

much older than you. It would never work between us."

"Who says it needs to work long-term? We have a few weeks. You're practically going to be glued to my side. We may as well enjoy ourselves."

"I don't want that."

"Are you sure?" Tabitha purred, leaning in close to speak in JK's ear, her soft breath sending shivers down JK's spine. She smelled like bergamot and something citrus. JK breathed in her scent for a second.

JK wasn't sure at all. What her body wanted and what her mind wanted were entirely different. JK's body was responding to Tabitha and Tabitha was clearly noticing that. JK had never been able to hide her feelings very well, and Tabitha was... Well, she was divine. Her pale skin was set off perfectly by her dark mussed hair and bright green eyes. Her nipples were showing through her crop top and that drove JK wild.

Tabitha was right about one thing—JK wanted her. But JK hadn't lied, either. She didn't want to start something with Tabitha that she knew would be doomed from the start. She wanted more than a fling. She wanted a real relationship, with a grown up woman of a similar age to her and Tabitha couldn't offer her that, for a number of reasons.

Her body may want Tabitha, but her mind was screaming at her to put the brakes on, and JK was not in the habit of letting her body's reactions overwhelm logical thought. That's not how she had survived her time in the military and that's not how she was going to navigate this, either.

"I am your bodyguard, Tabitha. I think it's best that we keep things professional between us, nothing more."

Tabitha wasn't leaving it at that. "Maybe I could change your mind on that..."

"Bacon and eggs, Ma'am..."

JK sighed in relief as Dan came in, carrying two steaming plates piled high with bacon and scrambled eggs and fresh tomatoes on the vine. Tabitha pulled away from JK to take her plate, though not before Dan saw her practically hanging off JK. To his credit, he didn't react, putting down their food and leaving with a cheerful, "Enjoy your breakfast!"

"We should eat," JK said softly.

"Yeah. We've got a busy day ahead of us."

"Is that right?"

"Yeah. I want to go see a movie, then go out to dinner at a fancy restaurant."

Those sounded safe enough, so JK didn't protest. "Alright, then. Tell me when you're ready to go."

"Aren't you going to help me pick out what to wear?"

"It's just a movie and dinner, Tab. You can wear whatever you want. Besides, I'm sure you know much better than me in matters of fashion."

"It's not just dinner, it'll be dinner at the most exclusive restaurant around. I'd like your feedback."

It was on the tip of JK's tongue to tell Tabitha that she should just ask Alice for fashion advice, but Tabitha looked so hopeful that JK couldn't bring herself to say no.

"Fine, but if you end up looking ridiculous after taking my advice, that's on you."

"I bet I won't look ridiculous. Give yourself more credit, JK."

JK sighed. This job was far from easy for very different reasons than one might expect.

JK hoped that Tabitha didn't dress her in anything too stupid-looking for dinner, but what she was wearing was honestly low on her list of priorities. She cared about keeping Tabitha safe, and the last thing she needed was to have Tabitha decide that JK was the enemy. She needed to stay in Tabitha's good books and keep her cooperation.

Gray had told JK some stories about bodyguards who had uncooperative clients. It sounded truly awful, and JK had no intention of being one of those cautionary tales. Luckily, Tabitha, despite her high standing, didn't seem to have a difficult nature.

They finished eating and JK followed Tabitha up to her room. Tabitha's wardrobe was... intimidating. She had bought half the store yesterday, and that didn't even come close to comparing to what she'd brought with her.

"I can see why you need help choosing," JK muttered.

"Exactly! Usually I have three people planning my outfits, but I guess for now, you'll have to do."

"I suppose I will. How about that blue dress? That's pretty."

"Hm, I'm not sure about that. It's more of a lunchtime formal dress than an evening formal dress."

JK had no idea how Tabitha could tell the

difference, but she just went with it. "Alright, which ones are the evening formal dresses?"

Tabitha started to pull out dresses... and dresses... and yet more dresses.

"How many evening functions did you intend on going to?" JK couldn't resist asking.

Tabitha just shrugged. "I like to be prepared for anything."

"So do I—perhaps prepared for different things. Tell me, Tab, if we were attacked right now and I told you to grab some essentials and run, would you know what to take?"

"Well, I suppose I'd take my purse, some clothes, shoes, toiletries, that kind of thing."

"Really? Which clothes, exactly? Which shoes and purse? Keep in mind that you have about thirty seconds here."

Tabitha stared hopelessly around the monstrous walk-in wardrobe. "I, uh... Well, I guess you're right. I'm not really prepared to run at a moment's notice. Do I need to be?"

JK sighed. "No, I suppose not. There is no significant risk to you while nobody knows who you are. It's just not what I'm used to."

Just another reminder that anything between her and Tabitha was a bad idea. JK had never met anyone as different from her as Tabitha was. Opposites may attract, but the things that made them opposites tended to drive them apart.

"Well, these are the evening gowns. What do you think?"

JK had no idea what criteria she was supposed to be judging this on, so she just picked something she thought was pretty.

"That green one." The emerald green satin would match perfectly with Tabitha's eyes, which was probably why Tabitha had bought it in the first place.

"Perfect! Then you can wear this green shirt with this black blazer and pants and we'll match."

"Great."

"Don't sound so enthusiastic, JK."

"I'm totally enthusiastic!"

"Yeah, right."

JK couldn't quite hide a smile and Tabitha giggled. Her giggles were endearing and JK felt herself being drawn in again.

Stop it. She is so young.

"Okay, we'll be casual for the movie, and we can stop back here to get dressed for dinner. Do you know what movies are on right now?"

"No, but I can google it."

"Nah, let's just see when we get there. I'm sick of living my life online. I have to do that at home—that or get mobbed whenever I leave the palace. Here, I want to go out and experience everything the world has to offer."

It wasn't fair that Tabitha had to deal with all this. She was so young. She should be allowed to explore the world freely, but circumstances had robbed her of that.

"Then I guess we're going back to that damn mall."

"Don't worry, it'll grow on you."

"Yeah, like a tumor."

Tabitha giggled again and held out her hand. JK took it without thinking, and by the time she realized what she had done, it seemed too late to take it back. The two of them walked hand-in-hand through the house and out to the car, where Jack was already waiting for them.

"Good morning, Ma'am."

"Hey, Jack."

"Hi, Jack! We'd like to go back to the mall, please."

"Right away, Princess."

"Tabitha."

"Yes, Princess Tabitha."

JK hid her smile as Tabitha pouted. She was adorable.

They got to the mall and headed for the movie theater. Tabitha looked at the different movie posters while JK watched the people around them.

"What do you want to watch, JK?"

"Anything you want. It's your trip, after all."

"We should at least try to find something that we'll both like. Take a look at the offerings."

JK reluctantly wrenched her eyes from the crowd and started perusing the posters, listening keenly to the surrounding conversations even as she allowed her eyes to wander.

"Hello, ma'am. May I take a moment of your time, please?"

"How can I help you?" Tabitha asked. JK glanced back to see that she had moved off to the popcorn stand and quickly abandoned the movie posters to get closer to Tabitha.

"I was just wondering if you know how to work this? It's new and I'm not really sure how to log in..."

JK caught a glimpse of the man talking to Tabitha and hurried her pace. Something wasn't right about him, and she'd learned not to ignore her gut feelings.

Tabitha leaned in to look at the phone he was holding out and he struck, grabbing for her purse. Tabitha squeaked in alarm as he snatched the purse out of her hands and turned to run—right into JK.

"I believe that doesn't belong to you."

"What are you going to do about it, bitch?" he snarled, drawing himself up to his full height. He was bigger and taller than JK, but that didn't matter.

She didn't bother to answer him. Instead, she grabbed his jacket and pulled. He was heavy enough that it was difficult to pull him toward her, but that didn't matter either; she pulled herself to him instead.

Once she was close enough, she spun him and wrenched one of his arms up his back. With her other hand, she grabbed Tabitha's purse back.

Mall security swarmed in on them. JK lifted her hands, pointing to the man who was now shouting from the ground. "He was trying to steal. I was just getting my friend's purse back."

"Oh, don't worry, we know. This one here has been banned from the mall before. I don't know how he got past us, but he won't do so again. Come on, you."

JK turned to Tabitha as the thief was hauled away. "Are you alright?"

Tabitha nodded, her green eyes wide with admiration. "That was so hot."

JK chuckled. She didn't seem too traumatized, at least. "Let's get ourselves inside, hm?" They had drawn a small crowd of onlookers, and JK didn't want people looking too closely at Tabitha. "Have you decided what you want to watch?"

"Yeah, I think so."

They paid for tickets for some romance movie whose name was as unmemorable as its poster and hurried inside.

"Wait, JK, I want to get popcorn."

JK hesitated. She wanted to get Tabitha out of sight as soon as possible, but she understood that movies just weren't movies without popcorn.

"Fine but be quick about it."

Tabitha bought her popcorn with little fuss and the two of them gained the relative privacy of the movie theater.

"You need to be less trusting, Tab," JK said quietly. "That guy was clearly just trying to get close enough to snatch your bag."

"Well, obviously I didn't know that, or I wouldn't have let him get close."

Tabitha's naïveté may be endearing at times, but right now it was more infuriating than anything else. How was JK supposed to take care of her when she couldn't recognize even the most basic of threats on her own? It was just like that escort last night. Tabitha had no concept of people not being exactly who they said they were, and it was problematic.

"You're angry with me, aren't you?"

"No, I'm not angry," JK said truthfully. "I'm just coming to realize that this job may be a little more difficult than I originally bargained for, but that's for me to deal with. It's not really your problem. You're the client, after all."

"I don't want to be a nightmare client who makes your job more difficult. I didn't know he was up to no good, I swear."

"I know, Tab—I know you weren't doing it on purpose. Let's just move past it."

"Agreed."

Tabitha took JK's hand again, and JK couldn't bring herself to take it back. What was a little hand-holding in the grand scheme of things? It's not like Tabitha was making a marriage proposal. She just needed to keep her head and stay professional.

She only needed to hold out a few weeks. After that, Tabitha would be back in the UK, and the delicious temptation she provided would be removed from JK's sight.

For some reason, the thought provided JK with little comfort.

"It's late. We should go to bed." JK made no move to get up. She was so enjoying talking to Tabitha that she didn't want to leave, and Tabitha didn't seem at all inclined to kick her out.

"Not yet, JK. I'm on holiday, remember. No boring functions to go tomorrow, no one demanding my time."

"I'm not on holiday."

"Yeah, but you're guarding me, which means you need to be awake at the same hours I am. It's in your best interests to go to bed at the same time as me and wake when I do, so that you can follow me around as long as I'm awake."

She had a point there. Even though it was horrendously late, JK felt no desire to go to bed.

When she met Tabitha two weeks ago, she would have said that they would have nothing to talk about, but she would now be eating her words.

She and Tabitha had long conversations about everything from philosophy to politics to books. Tabitha had a fascinating brain and JK just loved to pick it.

"Tell me again about your coming out."

It was something they had discussed before, but JK understood why Tabitha kept coming back to the subject. "Well, most of my friends and family were accepting. One aunt and two friends, not so much. They didn't so much object in principle as they didn't take it seriously. They told me it was a phase and I would get over it, and that I just needed to find the right guy."

"What changed their minds?"

"Time, I guess—that and a stern talking-to once or twice. People can accept a lot when it's someone they love. I mean, you'll always get irredeemable bigots, but they're becoming fewer and fewer nowadays, I think."

"I hope you're right," Tabitha murmured.

JK wondered if Tabitha would finally say what was on her mind. She waited patiently, giving her time to think. So far, when this moment had come in the past, Tabitha had always changed the subject, but not this time.

"JK... I'm a lesbian too, you know." Her big green eyes were earnest as she said it.

JK had figured out as much herself, given the scene she had witnessed on her first day guarding Tabitha, and Tabitha's persistent attempts to charm her but she didn't want to interrupt, so she kept silent.

"I've known since I was twelve, but I've been too scared to come out because of who I am. Everyone expects me to marry a man and produce heirs, to continue the royal line, but I can't do that. The thought of being with a man makes me sick. I don't know how much longer I'll be able to avoid being matched up with a suitable guy without coming out, but I'm not sure if I even want to come out.

"I know coming out isn't easy for anyone, but for me... the whole world will be watching. Every bigot who wants a say will aim their vitriol at me. I'm not sure if I can handle that."

JK reached over and took Tabitha's hand. "I wish I could say something to make it better, but you're probably right. It is harder for you than for everyone else. I can only encourage you to be yourself. You're so bright and beautiful, Tab, just as you are. Others will see that, even if it does take them a bit of time to adjust. You're strong, too, more than you think—strong enough to handle whatever the world throws at you."

"You think so?"

"I know so."

"Thanks, JK. You're... I really appreciate everything you've done for me." Tabitha leaned in close and JK didn't stop her. Her heart was full of affection, and she didn't want Tabitha to stop.

Tabitha was back in her skimpy PJs and as much as their conversation was intense, JK couldn't stop her gaze straying to Tabitha's breasts again.

"It's been my pleasure."

The next thing she knew, JK found herself leaning in towards Tabitha and their lips met. Tabitha's lips were soft and tasted sweet, like strawberries. JK swiped her tongue along Tabitha's lower lip before pulling it into her mouth. Tabitha moaned softly and surged forward, wrapping an arm around JK's neck.

Reality came crashing down around JK's ears.

What was she doing?

She was kissing Tabitha.

Princess Tabitha. The 28 year old daughter of the Queen of England.

She couldn't do this. It was madness.

She regretfully pulled back. Tabitha tried to chase her lips, but JK gently put a hand on her shoulder to hold her back.

"I'm so sorry, Tab. That was inappropriate. It won't happen again, I promise."

"Don't promise that. I liked it." Tabitha was all wide eyes and innocence.

JK smiled sadly at her. "I think it's time for me to go to bed now."

She rolled off the couch she and Tabitha were reclining on and left, closing the door softly behind her. Tabitha's disappointed eyes made her desperately want to turn around but she managed to resist.

JK tried to shake off the feeling of bliss that the kiss had left. She shouldn't be feeling bliss right now. She should be horrified by what she had done, but it had felt so right.

Of course, no matter how right it had felt, reality wouldn't oblige her feelings. Tabitha was a princess, and in a few weeks she would be going back to the U.K. to live her life among other royalty.

If JK started something with her now, she was one hundred percent guaranteed to get her heart broken and most likely Tabitha's too. Even if they agreed it would be just sex, when there was sex, feelings tended to get involved, and JK didn't want to risk that.

She fell into bed and tried to go to sleep, but she tossed and turned for what felt like hours before she finally drifted off.

5

TABITHA

Tabitha stared after JK, still slightly dazed. That kiss had been... That should have been her actual first kiss. It had been everything she'd ever dreamed of—sweet and slow and fifty shades of hot. Most importantly, it had been with someone who she knew genuinely cared about her.

She was sure JK had enjoyed the kiss, if her widely dilated pupils as she pulled away were anything to go by. But JK clearly thought there were things more important than their mutual enjoyment—like boring professionalism.

Inappropriate, she'd said. Well, Tabitha would show her inappropriate. Now that she knew what kissing JK was like, she was determined to get more of it. She didn't know how to seduce anyone, but she sure as hell was going to try. Until JK told Tabitha that she didn't want her anymore, Tabitha would try.

There was no point in trying that tonight, though, not when JK's guard was up. Best to let her sleep and start the seduction attempts in the morning.

Tabitha was exhausted and fell asleep easily. When she slept, she dreamed of JK.

The next morning, they shared breakfast as usual. "I want to go shopping today."

"Again? Okay then. A different mall this time?"

They had been mall hopping for the past two weeks. This time, it didn't matter to Tabitha which one they went to, but she decided not to let on what she was up to so early on in the game. "Yeah, that would be great."

They drove for an hour to get to a mall they hadn't visited before. Tabitha took them through a series of stores—bookstores, jewelry stores and clothing stores—before finally coming to where she wanted: a shop that specialized in lingerie.

"How do you think this would look on me?" she asked JK innocently, holding up a lacy pink bra.

JK went the same shade of pink as the bra. "I'm sure it'll look lovely."

"Come on, I want your feedback."

JK reluctantly waited outside the changing room while Tabitha changed. Tabitha had her sexiest panties on—black lace that hugged her curves in a way she was sure would drive JK wild.

She pranced out of the changing room in nothing but her panties and the bra she was trying on.

"Tabitha! Get back inside," JK hissed.

"There's no one around, silly."

JK took her arm and pulled back into the changing room, which suited Tabitha just fine. She turned to face JK, fully aware of how close they were now. "So, what do you think?"

JK's eyes flicked down Tabitha's body and her face went from pink to red. "You look incredible. Now you should get dressed. Please."

"Sure thing. Let me just take this off." Tabitha moved a little to the left, standing between JK and the door. Then she took the bra off, letting her breasts spring free. JK gulped and stared for a moment before bringing her eyes to the ground.

Tabitha didn't move, she wanted JK to look at her with that hunger in her dark eyes again.

"I should go." JK wriggled past Tabitha and managed to get to the door. She quickly left, closing the door behind it. Tabitha screwed her face up. She was sure JK wanted her. Why wouldn't she just give in to it?

JK had pulled her mask of professionalism back on by the time Tabitha got out of the changing room, but Tabitha was satisfied to know that she was having at least some effect on her.

She brushed past JK as she exited the changing room, letting herself linger for a few moments. JK closed her eyes but didn't pull away. Tabitha wanted to kiss her right now, but she suspected that if JK was to give in, she would not be doing so in a public changing room. Best to save her real attempts for at home, when they were alone.

The rest of the shopping trip passed smoothly, though Tabitha didn't miss an opportunity to pass close to JK or let her hand linger on JK's skin for just a few extra moments.

By the time they were in the car on the way home, JK was practically radiating waves of sexual frustration. Tabitha understood, because she felt similarly. She may have been doing everything she could think of to seduce JK, but it didn't come without its cost.

She was so horny she felt ready to explode and could think of little else but sex with JK. What would her first time be like? What would JK be like?

The moment they were inside, Tabitha moved to pin JK against the wall. She was certain JK could have prevented her from doing so, she was taller and stronger, but JK allowed herself to be pressed up against the wall, her chest heaving as she looked at Tabitha through heavily lidded eyes.

"I know what you're doing, Tab, and it's not going to work."

"Please, JK, I need you. I need you so badly."

JK's eyes were unreadable but her expression wavered, and Tabitha pressed her advantage.

"I need to feel your fingers inside me, JK. I need your tongue on me. I need you and I need you right now or I think I'm going to die. I've waited my whole life for this."

JK's moan of surrender was the hottest thing Tabitha had ever heard. Their lips crashed together and their tongues intertwined. JK pressed her knee between Tabitha's legs and Tabitha shamelessly rutted onto JK's knee, rubbing her clit against the source of divine pressure.

She broke away from the kiss to gasp for air,

but JK just kept kissing her, sucking wet kisses into her neck that Tabitha was sure were going to leave marks. She found she liked the idea of being marked by JK, of wearing JK's bruises on her skin.

Tabitha was working herself into a frenzy, rubbing against JK's knee. She was embarrassingly close to orgasm already and forced herself to pull back. No way was she coming against a *knee* when JK had so much more to offer.

"Bedroom," Tabitha gasped. JK lifted her off her feet and Tabitha wrapped her legs around JK's waist. JK walked them both to the bedroom, capturing Tabitha's lips once more as she did.

The next thing she knew, Tabitha was being laid down on the bed. She stared up at JK, realizing that she didn't know what to do now. She knew how sex worked, of course, but now that she was faced with actually doing it, she didn't know where to start.

Did she touch JK, or wait for JK to touch her? What exactly were they going to do? There were many ways for two women to have sex and Tabitha didn't know where to start.

JK must have read some of the anxiety off Tabitha's face, because she pulled back to look at her. "Is this alright, Tab?"

"It's more than alright. It's just that I've never done this before. I don't really know what I'm doing."

JK gave her a crooked grin. "Don't worry—I do. Just lie back and relax. I'll take care of you."

She didn't give Tabitha much more time to worry. JK started undressing her, pressing kisses to every inch of skin as it was revealed. By the time she was fully naked, Tabitha was writhing under JK's touch and soaking the bed beneath her.

"I need—JK... God, I need you... please..."

"Shh, I've got you, Tab. Just trust me."

JK started sucking gently on one of Tabitha's nipples. Tabitha gasped and arched her chest upward, encouraging JK to take more into her mouth. JK moved from one nipple to the other, sucking, licking and nibbling lightly.

It was very apparent that she knew exactly what she was doing. She was driving Tabitha crazy with lust and Tabitha didn't know how much more of this treatment she could withstand.

JK moved further down, teasing her with her fingers for what felt like forever before sliding one finger easily into her soaked pussy.

"Yes, yes, yes!" Tabitha rocked her hips against

JK's finger, drawing her in deeper. Tabitha had never felt anything this good.

JK chuckled. She added another finger, and Tabitha thought she was going to come right there. She was so close, but she couldn't quite tip over the edge. She knew that the moment she touched her clit, she would be gone.

She didn't want to do that, though. She wanted JK to make her come, so she waited.

JK twisted her fingers inside Tabitha and started stroking her G-spot. Tabitha wailed and trembled, her entire body tensing, right on the edge of coming and yet unable to tip over.

"JK—uh... oh god... uh..." She trailed off, babbling incoherently, reduced to a writhing mess under JK's ministrations.

"I'm going to lick your clit, Tabitha, but you're not going to come—not yet. I want to taste you thoroughly before you do, so you're going to hold off until I've had my fill, you understand?"

"I can't—I'm too close! JK, please..."

"If you're too close, then perhaps we should take a minute for you to cool off."

"NO! I need you now, JK!"

JK chuckled again. "Very well, but don't come. Not yet."

Tabitha tried to brace herself. *Don't come, don't come, don't come.*

It was no good. JK gave her clit a long, slow lick.

Tabitha screamed as her orgasm slammed into her. JK kept licking her, firm and slow, drawing out the orgasm impossibly long, until Tabitha thought she might die from the unending waves of pleasure drowning out everything else.

It finally ended, and JK pulled back, pressing kisses up her side and her neck, finally ending at her lips. Tabitha lay limply on the bed, catching her breath.

"Naughty girl," JK murmured. "I see we're going to have to teach you some control."

If she hadn't been so wrung out, the words would have sent a thrill of desire through Tabitha. As it was, her mind was already leaping forward into the future, wondering exactly how it was JK intended to teach her control.

Tabitha was aware that JK was still breathing harshly and her eyes were pooled wide with desire.

"Let me do it to you."

"I can take care of myself."

"I'm sure you can, but I want to try. I really really want to try."

JK looked in thought for a moment and then quickly undressed and lay back opening her legs.

Tabitha moved herself between them and began to kiss and lick at JK's hard abdomen before moving lower and feeling JK's body responding in light shivers.

Tabitha loved how JK was responding to her and moved her mouth lower trailing her tongue down to JK's pussy. She licked long and slow from bottom to top and JK moaned loudly.

Tabitha smiled to herself. She was doing it. She was making love to a woman, finally.

Tabitha repeated her action again and again, long, slow and teasing and she felt JK's wetness coating her tongue.

God, I love the taste of her. I could do this for hours.

But it took only seconds more before JK's orgasm came, as though from nowhere, exploding on Tabitha's tongue as her whole body tensed and her hand grabbed the back of Tabitha's head.

She felt shocked and happily surprised as she moved to lap at every last bit of JK's pleasure.

I did it.

She smiled to herself and raised her head meeting JK's relaxed happy gaze with her own.

She flopped down on the bed next to JK and pulled her in for a soft kiss. "That was... That was incredible, JK. I couldn't have asked for anything better for my first time."

"You certainly were persistent about getting what you wanted."

"Well, you certainly were stubborn about making sure I didn't get it."

"I guess you're the more stubborn of the two of us."

"Are you complaining?"

"Certainly not."

Tabitha wondered if JK had given in now, or if she would go back to resisting at every turn. She hoped it was the former. She was more determined than ever to pursue this thing with JK. She'd be mad to say no to something this good.

She wouldn't bring that up now, though. She was too content and relaxed to talk about serious stuff right now. All she wanted was to snuggle up to JK's side, which is exactly what she did. JK put an arm around her, and together, the two of them drifted off.

6

JK

JK watched Tabitha as she slept. She was tired, but she couldn't sleep yet. Her mind was buzzing with too many conflicting thoughts to allow her to rest.

What she'd just done with Tabitha... while she knew logically that she should regret it, she couldn't bring herself to do so. She'd had plenty of good sex in her life, but nothing had ever approached that. It wasn't just the sex, either. She was drawn to Tabitha in a way she had never been drawn to anyone else.

JK knew that she was walking a dangerous line, but she was in too deep just to walk away. There was really only one thing to do.

JK woke early the next morning to find Tabitha

still sleeping peacefully next to her, nestled into her side. She didn't look like she'd moved all night, expect perhaps to snuggle closer to JK. She was so cute, JK just couldn't wake her.

She gently extracted herself from Tabitha to use the bathroom and hesitated on her way back. She wanted to crawl back into bed with Tabitha and kiss her as she woke up, but JK knew that would be a bad idea. If they were going to do this, they would have to keep emotions as separate as they could be, which meant no more sleeping in the same bed.

JK regretfully returned to her own room and showered. By the time she was out, she could hear movement from Tabitha's room. Instead of going straight to her like she wanted to, JK forced herself to check on the security cameras. Tabitha's safety came before anything else.

Everything looked clear, so JK finally allowed herself to go to Tabitha, who was sitting on the edge of her bed, brushing her hair, looking like the vision of beauty she was.

"You left," Tabitha looked up at her with big sad eyes as JK stepped inside.

"I did." JK came to sit down next to Tabitha.

"Tab, if we're going to do this, then there have to be some rules."

"So we're going to keep doing this, then?" Tabitha's lovely green eyes were suddenly sparkling with excitement as she looked up at her, and it was impossible not to get caught up in it.

"Yes, well, I think we've already established that I can't resist you... But you need to understand that we're from completely different worlds. A romantic relationship between us would never work. We can have sex—as much sex as you would like—but it can't be more than that. We can't get feelings involved, and when your holiday ends, you will go back to your life in England, leaving me as nothing more than a pleasant memory."

The thought of Tabitha leaving made JK's chest ache, which just went to show exactly how careful she needed to be with this issue.

"If that's the way it has to be, then that's what we'll do."

JK looked at Tabitha in surprise. She had expected more push-back than that and couldn't deny that she was a little disappointed. As much as she knew there could never be more, she couldn't hide her disappointment that more was all she wanted.

Still, this was the only way it could work. She reminded herself that she was fortunate that Tabitha was going along so easily.

"Great. Then in that case, how about I give you a proper good morning?"

JK wound a hand into Tabitha's loose bed hair and pulled her in for a kiss. The two of them kissed lazily for a minute, but the kiss started to heat up in no time. Tabitha's lips were like gasoline to the fire that was burning inside JK.

As amazing as the sex had been last night, Tabitha was so alluring that it didn't take long for JK's body to wake up and start demanding things like her tongue inside Tabitha's pussy. She moaned at the thought and was about to act on it when Tabitha's stomach growled.

JK pulled away, grinning. "I guess it's time for breakfast."

"We can have breakfast... if we can come back here for dessert."

Fuck, she is so beautiful.

Her lips were swollen and red from the kissing.

JK gave Tabitha one last lingering kiss. "Whatever my princess commands."

They ate breakfast in record time and practically raced back to the bedroom, past a scandalized Alice, who JK was sure saw some of their clothes coming off before the door closed, but she didn't care about that right now.

All she cared about was tasting as much of Tabitha as was humanely possible. JK pushed Tabitha onto the bed and crawled between her legs, finding her already starting to get wet. She lapped up the wetness at Tabitha's pussy, loving the taste of her.

"I never got to taste you properly last night. We're going to change that. But first, you need to be punished."

"P-punished?" Tabitha looked confused but there was a light of intrigue in her eyes.

"I told you not to come until I was done with you, and you came anyway. I want you over my lap, ass up. I'm going to spank you."

JK positioned herself so that she was sitting on the edge of the bed and as Tabitha wriggled into position. She paused, needing confirmation. "Tab? Is this okay?"

"Yes, please," she gasped. "I want to try."

"You just say if its too much and I'll stop, ok?"

Tabitha nodded, "Yes. OK."

JK brought her hand down onto Tabitha's ass, making the room ring with the sound of the slap.

Tabitha squeaked in surprise and gripped JK's ankles to stabilize herself.

"Are you still good?"

"Still good—keep going!"

"Say *red* if you want me to stop."

"I'm green, JK."

JK paused in surprise. She wouldn't have thought Tabitha would know about safe words.

"I read books, okay? Many many books! Just get on with it and spank me already!"

JK brought her hand down again on Tabitha's ass. It was the most delightful feeling, having all that firm flesh under her palm, watching it slowly redden as she spanked Tabitha again and again. It wasn't too hard, it was rhythmical and JK enjoyed watching Tabitha's body respond.

Tabitha started moaning and rocking against JK's leg. JK grinned and spanked a little harder, drawing out another moan.

"JK, wait. Can we try something?"

"Of course."

JK let Tabitha get up off her lap and watched as she went over to a drawer. She got out a vibrating butterfly and strapped it over her clit before bringing herself back over JK's lap.

"Tab, you naughty girl. This is supposed to be a

punishment." JK smiled to herself. Everything about Tabitha's wide eyed innocence and puppy dog excitement just melted her.

"Please, JK? It feels so good. I want to come like this."

"How can I refuse you anything?" JK sighed. "Alright, then. Come, if you can, but I'm only giving you twenty strokes to do it."

Tabitha whined softly but didn't otherwise protest. JK started spanking again, harder this time and leaving slightly more time in between hits. Tabitha was gasping and writhing against her. JK could feel the butterfly vibrating against her leg and could only imagine how good it must feel against Tabitha's clit as Tabitha pressed tighter against her leg.

"Are you going to come, Tabitha?" She spanked Tabitha's ass again, hard. "Are you going to come for me, lying spread over my lap like this?"

"Yes!" Tabitha moaned. "Mmm... yes!"

"You've got two more spanks left. If you don't come after those, I'm going to take you off my lap and take the vibrator off you. You'll have to wait."

"No! I'm so close, please, JK!"

"We'll see."

JK delivered her last two strokes in quick

succession. Tabitha screamed and convulsed on JK's lap as she came hard, she pulsed and gushed liquid onto JK's leg, but JK didn't care about that. The sight of Tabitha coming was so hot it nearly had her undone.

Tabitha went limp over JK's lap, panting. JK stroked her red ass lightly. "That was so fucking hot."

"Yeah," Tabitha agreed weakly. She let JK help her up and laid back down on the bed, wincing slightly as she tried to lie on her back and her ass hit the mattress. She turned onto her side instead.

"Nuh-uh. On your back. I'm not done with you yet. You're going to come again before I'm done with you."

"JK, I can't. I've never come that hard in my life. It'll take me weeks to recover."

"We'll see about that."

JK started kissing Tabitha's neck, sucking marks around the marks that were already there. She loved marking Tabitha, and judging by the noises Tabitha was making, Tabitha loved it just as much. JK grinned. So much for needing weeks to recover.

She moved from Tabitha's neck down to her breasts, licking lightly before pulling one nipple into her mouth. She sucked on it, flicking her tongue over the tip, teasing with a light pressure until Tabitha moaned in frustration.

Only then did JK reward her with a firmer pressure. Tabitha was panting in earnest now and JK ran an experimental hand through her folds. Tabitha shivered and moaned, her wrist coming to JK's and guiding JK's hand to her clit.

JK rubbed it a few times before dipping her fingers lower, pushing them into Tabitha and finding her G-spot.

"This time, you're going to come from just my fingers inside you. No pressure on your clit at all."

"B-but I can't! That's not possible."

JK gave her a wicked grin. "Oh, Tabitha, I have a lot to teach you about what is and isn't possible."

Tabitha was so wet and open, JK easily added a third finger, causing Tabitha to arch up in pleasure into the touch. "Do you trust me?"

"Yes... totally," she moaned.

"We'll go slow. Tell me if anything hurts."

JK played for a minute with three fingers inside Tabitha, slowly moving them around deep inside her wetness. Tabitha's body was responding and she looked lost in pleasure as JK teased her. She slowly pushed a slippery fourth finger inside and Tabitha easily took it.

She took her time and played again, moving her fingers around deep within Tabitha. Tabitha was so wet and open for them and she kept pushing her hips towards JK.

"You want more?" JK asked.

Tabitha responded with moans and murmured "Yes, please."

JK pulled out for a second to rub the rest of her hand in Tabitha's wetness to make sure she was adequately coated in wetness, then she tucked her thumb into her palm and began to press her hand into Tabitha. It caught slightly at the knuckles and she lowered her mouth to Tabitha's clitoris to lick her slowly yet firmly as she pressed in further, and her whole hand slid inside Tabitha past her knuckles. Tabitha gasped sharply and JK paused where she was.

"Am I hurting you?"

"No, it feels good, JK. So good."

"You want me to keep going?"

Tabitha opened her eyes and lifted her head for a second and nodded, before relaxing her head back onto the pillow. Her whole body was relaxed and open in front of her. JK admired the way her lovely full breasts ran down to her narrow waist and then her hips opened out in front of her.

JK watched, mesmerized, as her hand slowly disappeared up to the wrist in Tabitha's body. She could feel the sides of Tabitha's pussy contracting around her as she made a fist and started moving it very slowly deep inside.

Tabitha was moaning and moving her body slowly as though in a trance. JK knew that being stretched and filled so much could take you to another world and it looked like Tabitha was there now.

"Oh—oh, that's so good. I feel so *full*,"

"You look so beautiful, Tab. You feel so good on my hand."

JK began to move her fist slowly against Tabitha's G spot and then gradually quicker. Tabitha was responding and moaning and writhing and JK felt her tighten around her hand.

Seconds later she felt Tabitha's orgasm clutching at her, running through her body which tightened and released. JK felt her gush against her hand.

She smiled and stilled her hand inside for a second as Tabitha came down from the orgasm slightly.

JK then dipped her head to Tabitha's clitoris and took her in her mouth licking slowly and sucking as she built Tabitha back up. Her hand was still deep inside Tabitha and she began to rock it slowly against Tabitha's G spot.

Tabitha's moans began to increase again and her hips began to rock themselves on JK's hand.

JK loved having this power and being able to give this level of pleasure to a woman, but somehow, it being Tabitha specifically made it feel all the more special. Tabitha's first time for everything and yet she was so sexual and so trusting and so open.

As JK began to suck gently on Tabitha's clitoris it tipped her over the edge. Tabitha screamed as she came again, gushing inside against JK's hand and pulsing liquid that dribbled out onto the bed below her. JK kept her hand still deep inside until Tabitha's cry trailed off and her pussy stopped contracting.

JK released her fist and very slowly and carefully slid her hand out, causing Tabitha to whimper softly. JK kissed her until she was smiling rather than whimpering and lay down beside her. JK's body was thrumming with need and screaming for release, but she didn't know if

Tabitha would be up for anything else after what she had just been through.

Tabitha lay for a minute just recovering and breathing and JK watched her, entranced by her beauty.

Her hair was messy and her skin was pink from the orgasms. Her nipples were still hard and there were marks on her neck and breasts from JK's firm kisses. JK thought to herself that she had never seen anyone look so beautiful.

"You are incredible," she whispered. "You are the most beautiful woman I have ever seen."

Tabitha opened her eyes that were hazy and dark green with lust and looked up at her. JK wanted nothing more than to kiss her again. Kiss every single inch of her body and never ever stop.

Tabitha propped herself up on one elbow. "What do you want, JK? I want to make you feel good, too."

JK knew she could get off quickly and she wanted to.

"I want your fingers inside me."

Tabitha didn't need to be asked twice as she moved between JK's legs and pushed her fingers inside.

"Like this?" she asked innocently.

"Curl your fingers upwards to find my G spot." JK directed and showed her the action with her own hand in the air.

Tabitha watched intently and adjusted her fingers inside JK. JK could feel how wet she was and then she suddenly felt Tabitha's fingers hit her G spot.

"There," she gasped in pleasure and felt her head tip back. "Right there. Now kind of thrust in and out but keep your fingers in that position to hit that spot."

She caught sight of Tabitha's face, a look of intense concentration on it as her fingers began to thrust in and out of JK.

"Yes..." JK moaned. "Just like that. Now gradually increase your speed."

JK moved her right hand to her own swollen clitoris and used two fingers to massage herself. As Tabitha gradually increased the speed of her thrusts, JK increased the speed her own fingers were moving against her clitoris.

It was then only a matter of seconds before JK felt the crescendo of her orgasm crash over her in waves with a power she couldn't remember the last time she felt. She lay back in a heap, utterly dazed and left shuddering with the aftershocks of the orgasm.

The world faded out for a few moments in the wake of the strength of her pleasure. When she came back to herself, Tabitha had removed her fingers and was kissing her way up JK's side, all the way to her lips.

They exchanged a sticky, sated kiss before falling into bed together.

"That was the best dessert ever."

JK had to laugh at that. "I was always a sucker for chocolate mousse, but I have to admit, this is going to be my number one favorite dessert going forward."

"Any chance of second helpings?"

"Tabitha! We literally just finished! Are you seriously ready for round two already?"

"Not right now... but in half an hour or so... well, I might get hungry for something sweet again."

"We're not going to leave this bed all day, are we?"

"Nope," Tabitha said happily. "Probably not tomorrow either. The next day... we can maybe go out for a few minutes, just to get some fresh air."

"You're awful."

"You love it."

JK did. God help her, she really did.

JK checked the security cameras. She knew she was in trouble. Not because anything was wrong on the cameras—all was good on that front.

No, the mess she had gotten herself into was all internal. She had known it was a risk, but she had told herself that she wouldn't fall into this trap. And yet, here she was, falling for it anyway.

JK was falling for Tabitha and falling hard.

It was so much more than just frequent, hot sex. She loved Tabitha's sparkling personality and her wide-eyed innocence. JK hoped that she never lost that. JK needed someone like Tabitha in her life, someone to keep her from taking things too seriously and remembering that life was wonderful.

She thought that Tabitha could use someone like her in her life, too—someone grounded and practical, who could take care of her and shoot down some of her crazier ideas.

No, JK was not going to go along this line of thought again. It was too dangerous.

She and Tabitha could never be in a real relationship. Tabitha was a princess, for fuck's sake! It would *never* work between them, and she needed to remind herself of that.

She probably didn't even really have feelings for Tabitha. All the sex they were having—and it was a lot of sex—was probably making her body go haywire with chemicals that mimicked real feelings. That had to be all it was.

Some small part of JK knew she was just fooling herself, but she shoved that part away and clung tenaciously to her brain chemicals excuse. It was all she had to work with, so she was going to make it work.

"J! There you are."

JK almost winced. Did Tabitha's eyes really have to light up that way when they saw each other? It made JK's heart flutter in a warm and pleasant way, and poked great big holes in her not-falling-for-Tabitha mantra.

"Sorry, did I wake you?" In the three weeks since she and Tabitha had been sleeping together, JK had relented on the rule that they weren't to sleep in the same bed. It was only practical, after all, she told herself.

Often, after sex, they were both too tired to be

moving to separate beds. It made sense to share the same bed. And if JK enjoyed falling asleep with Tabitha curled up next to her, well, that was just a happy coincidence.

"No, you're just rubbing off on me. I'm waking earlier and earlier. It's unnatural, I swear."

"The early bird catches the worm."

"Yeah, right. More like, *the early bird catches Tab's unsuspecting pussy.*"

JK snorted a laugh. She had taken to waking Tabitha with oral sex. Tabitha was getting truly spoiled—she would pout on the morning she wasn't woken by JK's tongue on her and insist that JK make up for it after breakfast. JK was only too happy to oblige.

"Hardly unsuspecting anymore, hm? Why don't you go back to bed, love? It's still early for you, and we both know you get cranky if you don't get your beauty sleep. I'll wake you properly in an hour or two."

Tabitha was looking at her funny. JK frowned, wondering what she'd said. She went over it in her head and suddenly felt her face going red as she realized the endearment she had let slip without realizing it.

"Go on, to bed with you, *Tabitha.*"

"Fine, fine, I'm going."

Tabitha shot JK a lingering look over her shoulder before leaving. JK shook herself slightly. It didn't mean anything. Just a slip of the tongue. That's all it was.

She wondered if she'd have to explain that to Tabitha. Hopefully not. She didn't want to hurt Tabitha's feelings and fervently hoped that they could leave this little incident behind them.

JK did a quick patrol of the property to clear her head, but everything was calm. This was certainly an easy job, at least in terms of body-guarding. In other areas... Well, it certainly had its challenges.

As she was walking back to Tabitha's room, she ran into Alice, who was taking an armful of sheets to the wash with a look of distaste on her face. JK didn't blame her; those sheets were soaked with the aftermath of their pleasure.

"What are you doing?" Alice asked sharply as JK moved to open Tabitha's door.

"Tabitha asked me to wake her."

"I can do that!"

"I'm sure you can, but she asked me to," JK said evenly. Alice had been extremely difficult ever since finding out that JK and Tabitha were being intimate. JK was sure it was only because she was concerned for Tabitha.

After all, Alice must know as well as she and Tabitha did that this thing between them couldn't last. Alice was probably only worried for Tabitha's heart once this holiday was over and she and JK said their goodbyes.

The knowledge of that inevitable moment felt like a crouching monster, waiting to pounce on JK as she moved inevitably toward it. Neither she nor Tabitha had discussed the date of her departure, which was yet to be set. They were both avoiding the subject, and JK was content to avoid it for the foreseeable future.

Alice grumbled under her breath and stomped off with the sheets. JK sighed. Alice's attitude was unfortunate, but there was nothing to be done about it.

JK quietly let herself into the room and got between Tabitha's legs, letting Alice slip from her mind. She was exactly where she wanted to be, and she wasn't going to let anyone else tell her otherwise.

"I want to go to a movie."

"A movie," JK said flatly.

"Don't look at me like that! It won't be like the last one."

"Really? Because in the last one, I seem to remember us getting kicked out by the manager halfway because you were moaning too loudly while I touched you."

"Hey, I didn't see you complaining!"

"Because I'm an idiot, admittedly, but you still started it!"

"I'm not going to start anything this time, I promise."

"Fine, then I guess we can go to a movie."

JK let Tabitha pick the movie and the two of them got as comfortable as they could in the movie theater seats. Tabitha's hand moved to JK's thigh, but she didn't do anything other than give it a gentle squeeze.

After the movie was done, the two of them wandered through the mall for a while, buying things here and there. Tabitha's love of shopping would forever confound JK, but she viewed it with tolerant fondness rather than the exasperation she had felt at first.

They were just exiting into the parking lot

when JK was caught by surprise by a passing woman.

"Are you? You are aren't you? Princess Tabitha?" The woman was intense and grabbed Tabitha's arm. For once Tabitha was outside without her big sunglasses on. She had also stopped wearing the brown contact lenses religiously and her hair was beginning to grow. They had gotten too comfortable and it had backfired on them.

"Oh my god! Wow!" The woman's voice hit a higher pitch. "I'm such a huge royal family fan! Could I get a photo? Please?" She raised her phone.

JK moved swiftly and firmly to cover the woman's phone and push her hand down. "I'm really sorry that won't be possible," she said and Tabitha just looked shocked and saddened by what was happening.

Luckily at that point their car swung around the corner and pulled up in front of them.

JK opened the back door and immediately shepherded Tabitha in, separating her from the intense woman. She got in the car next to Tabitha and pulled the door closed.

She took a deep breath. They were safe.

Tabitha was shaken, but her cover was somewhat blown. Who knew who this woman would try and tell?

Jack drove them back to the mansion in silence and Tabitha leaned into JK and JK held her the whole way.

There was an unfamiliar man in a suit waiting for them on the mansion steps. JK stiffened, readying herself to defend Tabitha, but Tabitha stepped confidently out of the car, walking right up to him. "Richard, what are you doing here?"

7

TABITHA

Tabitha didn't know why her uncle was here, but she was still pleased to see him. She was shaken from the events of earlier and the sight of a family member was welcome.

"Tabitha," he said stiffly, "I'm here to take you home."

Tabitha frowned. "What?"

"I'm here to take you home."

"My holiday isn't done yet. What are you talking about?"

"You know exactly what I'm talking about. Your inappropriate behavior has reached your mother, and she commands you to return with me."

"My inappropriate behavior?" Tabitha's mind was spinning. She and JK hadn't exactly been subtle, but she had thought they were safe, half a world away from her family. Of course, she knew they wouldn't take news of the affair well, but she had never intended to tell them.

How had they found out? There was no way, unless... Alice. Tabitha felt anger lick her insides. Of course, Alice had betrayed her. She had made no secret of her disapproval of what JK and Tabitha were doing. When it came down to it, she had chosen to be loyal to her mother and not Tabitha.

Tabitha folded her arms. "I'm not leaving, and you can't make me."

"Oh, I believe you will find that I can."

JK took an aggressive step forward. "I believe she has given you her answer."

"You stay out of this! You have no right to speak here."

"Don't talk to J like that!"

"This woman has corrupted your mind, Tabitha! I am removing you from her influence at once."

"No, you're not, and if you try to force me, I *will*

make a fuss. I'll turn this into an international incident. I'll go to the U.S. embassy for asylum against homophobia if I must."

Richard went bright red. "This isn't about your preference for women, Tabitha—which, by the way, it would have been nice not to be blindsided with! This woman is your bodyguard and she's twice your age! If you want a woman, we can discuss that, but we'll find you an *appropriate* woman of the correct standing."

Some part of Tabitha was relieved that her sexuality was apparently a possibility, but mostly, she was angry. "J is appropriate! It is her I want. I'm in love with her."

"Tab," JK took her hand, "We always knew that this was going to end. He is right, there is no future for us, we are from different worlds. I don't want you to get into this kind of trouble over me. I'm not worth it."

"That's crap, J! You are worth everything! I love you." Tabitha knew in that moment that she really did love her.

"This isn't about homophobia and you know it, Tabitha. You have no grounds to seek asylum." Richard chimed in.

"The media won't see it that way. Do you really want to cause that type of uproar? Because if you try to force me home, I promise you I won't hesitate to do it."

Richard let out a sharp breath, his hands clenched into fists. "Fine, but *she's* not to protect you anymore!" Richard looked to JK. "You are officially fired. You may stay for a couple of hours to collect your stuff while I source a new *male* bodyguard. After that, I want you out of Tabitha's life for good, or there will be trouble for both of you."

JK lifted her head high. "Tabitha is an adult. She has the right to see whoever she wants, and you can't stop her."

"You're right. She has every right to defy her mother... and her mother has every right to disown her for it."

The blood drained from JK's face. "You can't do that!"

"Yes, we can. Tabitha will lose everything. She has no qualifications, no money in her own name. She won't ever be queen—she won't ever be anything. Her life will be in ruins."

Tabitha swayed on her feet. She was going to have to go along with this for now. She and JK would have to think of a plan once Richard was pacified. "Fine, I'll take another body-guard, Richard. Now will you please leave me the fuck alone? I believe J and I need to say goodbye."

Richard gave JK a withering look. "You have three hours."

JK and Tabitha walked into the house and closed the door. Tabitha peered through the curtains to be sure Richard was driving away before flinging her arms around JK, tears springing back to her eyes.

"J, what are we going to do?"

JK hugged her back tightly. "We always knew this was going to happen, Tab. I'll admit, I hoped we would have more time, but now that it's here, we'll just have to accept it."

Wait, what?

"What are you talking about?"

JK frowned. "I'm talking about the fact that we need to part ways."

"Are you mad? Did you seriously think I was accepting that? I was just saying that to get Richard off our backs for a while so that we could come up with a real plan!"

"Tabitha, there is only one realistic plan. We have to cut ties. Two people like you and me can't ever be together in the real world. We have been living in a bubble. They will never accept me."

Tabitha pulled back to look at JK. "What are you talking about?"

"I'm talking about you being disowned! I'm talking about an international scandal. I'm not going to let that happen. You'd lose everything."

"You *are* my everything, J!"

"You may say that now, but you don't understand the realities of the world everyone else lives in. You've lived an incredibly sheltered life. The real world would eat you alive."

Hurt bloomed in Tabitha's chest. "You think I can't handle it?"

"I think you shouldn't have to."

"What if I don't want to lose you?"

"That was always an inevitability."

Tabitha wanted to scream. She wanted to shake JK and demand that JK fight for her... but JK wouldn't and no amount of screaming or demanding would change her mind.

"Please, don't go," Tabitha whispered. "I..."

I love you.

She couldn't say that again now though. She had said it already in the heat of the moment and it hadn't made any difference to JK's decision. She wasn't going to put that on JK now again in an attempt to make her stay. When she said it again, she didn't want it to be part of a desperate attempt to keep JK. She wanted to say it knowing that JK was as committed to her as she was to JK.

"I'm so sorry, Tabitha, but this is the way it has to be. We said from the beginning that it was just sex."

Tabitha recoiled as though JK had hit her. "Is that really all I am to you? Just sex?"

"No," JK admitted. "No, I think we've gone past the point of denying that much... but we were both wrong to get feelings involved. It was always going to end in disaster. It's my fault. I should have been stronger. If I had resisted you from the beginning, none of this would have happened."

"This isn't your fault, JK! It's my stupid family and their stupid expectations!"

"Regardless of whose fault it is, this has to end. I'm sorry, Tabitha. I should pack up my stuff."

Tabitha stared stupidly after JK as she walked to her room, the room she hadn't used much recently since she had practically moved into Tabitha's room.

Tabitha wanted to run after her and beg her to stay, but what else could she say that she hadn't already said? She shuddered as a sob wracked through her body. How could this be happening?

Perhaps JK had been right. She had been foolish to delude herself into thinking that this could end any other way.

But that didn't mean she wouldn't fight it.

Tabitha wiped her tears away and strode through the corridors, bursting into JK's room.

"No! No, JK. This isn't going to stand. So, I'll be disowned. So what? I'll move in with you. I'll get a job. We can figure this out, together. Please, I'm willing to fight for us. You just need to be willing to fight too."

JK put down the toiletry bag she was holding and came to take both of Tabitha's hands in hers. "Tabitha, I am fighting for you in the best way I know how. When you love someone, you do what's best for them, even when it breaks your own heart in the process."

"You are what's best for me." Tabitha sobbed

"I know you think that, but you're wrong. We live in different worlds. I'm your first love, but that doesn't mean there aren't other loves out there for you. There are plenty of other women out there. I am sure your mother will find you someone wonderful who you can be with and not cause friction within your family."

It was like talking to a brick wall. JK had clearly already made her decision and Tabitha's pleas weren't doing anything to change it. Tabitha didn't know what else she could say.

She turned away, tears still streaming down her face.

"Goodbye, Tab," JK said softly.

Tabitha didn't say goodbye. She couldn't. She wasn't ready to say goodbye to JK; she never would be.

She walked woodenly down the hall and collapsed into bed.

A few minutes later, the door opened. Tabitha shot up, sure for a moment that it would be JK, having changed her mind and willing to fix everything.

It wasn't JK. It was Alice.

"You!"

"Don't worry, Ma'am. She is gone. She said she's going to wait outside until your new bodyguard arrives."

"Alice, did you or did you not tell my mother about JK and me?"

"I did, Ma'am. It was my duty. I—"

"You're fired."

"What?"

"You heard me. I don't understand how you even have the nerve to look surprised. You betrayed me."

"I was loyal to the crown."

"I don't want to hear it, Alice. If you're so loyal, I'm sure my mother will offer you another job, but you are no longer part of my personal staff. Get your stuff and get out of here. Tell Richard to book a flight back to the U.K. with you so that you can return with him."

"But, Ma'am,"

"I don't want to hear it, Alice! GO!"

Alice wisely went, leaving Tabitha with nothing but her shattered heart.

Maybe two hours later, there was another knock on the door. Tabitha couldn't help the stupid hope that flared within her at that sound.

Once more, however, it wasn't JK. This time, it was an unfamiliar man dressed in a suit.

"Princess Tabitha? My name is Peter. I'm your new bodyguard."

"Great," Tabitha said dully, falling back onto the bed. Was there even any point in staying in

America anymore? JK didn't want her, at least not enough to fight for her.

She couldn't bring herself to leave, though. Leaving would mean leaving JK behind forever, and Tabitha couldn't do that. Even if JK didn't want her, Tabitha couldn't bear to close the door between them permanently.

Maybe some small part of her was hoping that JK would change her mind. That part was probably foolish.

Tabitha knew JK well enough to know that she was fiercely determined to protect those she cared about. She had decided that being with her would be harmful to Tabitha, and Tabitha knew that JK loved her enough to want the best for her. JK loved her. And she loved JK. Wasn't love supposed to be enough?

She was deluded in thinking that being apart would be better for Tabitha, but as long as she held that delusion—and Tabitha had no idea how to break it—she would stay away, for what she thought was Tabitha's own good.

Tabitha sank into the blankets, pulling them over her head entirely, wishing she could believe that this whole thing was just some awful nightmare and she'd wake up in JK's arms.

This was no nightmare, though. This was her life now.

Facing life without JK felt like a living nightmare, and there was no way for Tabitha to wake up.

8

JK

JK felt like she was being torn in two. Her body was leaving the mansion, but her heart was saying behind, with Tabitha. The look on Tabitha's face when she realized that JK didn't intend to stay with her had nearly broken JK.

She had to stay strong, though, for Tabitha's sake. Tabitha needed her, even if it wasn't in the way she thought she did. She needed JK to be strong and walk away, because Tabitha certainly wasn't going to and one of them had to, to protect Tabitha's future.

It was so unfair. Why did Tabitha have to be royalty? If she had been anyone else, she and JK would have been free to be together, but their worlds had never been compatible.

JK had always known that, and she had done the one thing she swore she would never do. She had fallen in love with Tabitha.

Of course, it wouldn't have been fair to say that to Tabitha, not when she was leaving. The unsaid words felt like they were burning the back of her throat, but JK knew that it was a burn she would have to get used to, just like the ache of her broken heart.

She hesitated in the hallway, wondering if she should stop by Tabitha's room for one last goodbye, but decided that she couldn't risk it. If Tabitha asked her one more time to stay, JK feared that she would say yes, which would only lead to Tabitha's ruin.

So, she walked away, bitter tears running down her cheeks.

She got home and flopped onto the couch, unsure what to do now. She should probably do practical things like shop for groceries or at least unpack her suitcase, but she couldn't bring herself to do any of that. It felt like her life had stopped and to start moving again would be to leave Tabitha for good.

Tabitha was still in the U.S., though. She wasn't gone entirely. JK made her decision. While Tabitha was here, JK would protect her. She didn't know if the new bodyguard they hired would be any good —the market was unfortunately flooded with frauds—but regardless of his skills, she would follow from a distance and watch out for Tabitha.

By the time Tabitha returned home, perhaps JK would then be ready to accept her fate. For now, she couldn't bring herself to let go completely. She was probably just prolonging her pain, but the thought of never seeing Tabitha again made it difficult to breathe. She couldn't live with that.

With renewed purpose, JK got into her car and drove back toward the mansion. She was careful to park a few blocks away and walk the remaining distance. If she was spotted anywhere near there, it would cause trouble for Tabitha for sure. That was the last thing she wanted.

JK watched the house but wasn't surprised to see no one come in or out that day. She didn't imagine Tabitha was up to much right now. She would need time to grieve, but she would move on. She was young; she had her entire life ahead of her. Any woman would be crazy not to want to be with her.

JK was resigned to living the rest of her life with a broken heart, but she felt sure that Tabitha would find love and move on. She hoped that after a while, Tabitha would be able to look back on their time together with fondness. JK supposed she would never know if that came to pass or not.

JK stayed until late in the evening before finally driving home. She knew that the alarm system that was set at night was top-notch. Tabitha should be safe enough with that on. It was during the day, when the beams weren't on, that she would need watching.

The next day, JK returned.

Tabitha still didn't leave the house.

Every day for a week, JK came back, and Tabitha hadn't left the house. JK was going out of her mind with worry. What was wrong with Tabitha? Was she sick? There hadn't been any doctors coming or going. Even worse was the thought that she was too heartsick to leave her bed. JK had done that to her. She hadn't had a choice, but she still felt awful about it.

She knew that Tabitha had let herself get attached, just like JK had. Unlike JK, however, Tabitha seemed to have developed a notion that things could somehow work between them long-term. This must be doubly hard on her, and JK hated herself for it, but she knew it was for the best.

She jumped as her phone chimed and quickly looked around to make sure Peter wasn't nearby. JK had yet to see him patrol the property, which didn't give her much confidence in his skills, but she supposed that if Tabitha wasn't leaving her bed, Peter needn't do much more than hang out in the house.

Still, it would be prudent to ensure that there were no lurking threats. It was a good thing JK was on the case. She looked at her phone and her heart clenched. It was a message from Tabitha.

J, I can't do this. I've been trying, I swear I have, but I need you. Please, come back to me.

JK shoved her phone back into her pocket, because she knew that if she didn't, she would break and respond, telling Tabitha that she was coming and Tabitha didn't need to hurt anymore.

But if she did that, it would be just the beginning of Tabitha's hurting, so JK had to resist, no matter how much she wanted to fix Tabitha's pain.

Movement caught JK's eye. She quickly stepped back between the branches of two trees, observing without being seen. It was Peter—about time he went on a patrol!

He didn't seem to be patrolling, though. He had his phone out and came to a stop a short distance from JK before placing a call.

"Hi, it's Peter Langton, for Queen Mary's chief of staff. Yes, thank you. Hello. No, nothing new to report. She still hasn't left her bed. Dan has been bringing her meals in her room, but she has mostly refuses them. Yes, I've tried to convince her to go out, but she screamed at me to leave her alone. Thank you, sir, much appreciated. Tomorrow at the usual time? Perfect. Goodbye."

Anger swelled up in JK's chest, so quickly she felt like she might explode. She clenched her hands into fists, resisting with all her might the urge to punch Peter.

So, this was why he hadn't been patrolling. He wasn't really interested in protecting Tabitha; that's not what he had been hired for. He had been hired to spy on her.

Perhaps her mother thought she was safe

enough in her anonymity here, or maybe she presumed Peter could spy and guard at the same time, but Peter clearly had his priorities set.

Well, JK wasn't going to let Tabitha's safety slide just because her mother seemed to think that was acceptable. She would do Peter's job for him if she must.

Tabitha's presence in the U.S. had already been unmasked once. Word could get out, and if word got out, that could be dangerous for Tabitha.

JK's phone chimed again.

JK, I can see you read my message. Please respond. I need to know that you are ok.

JK sighed. She couldn't let Tabitha think something had happened to her; that would just be cruel.

Tabitha, I'm fine. Sweetheart, I know it hurts, but you need to stop contacting me. A clean break will be better for both of us. You know it can't happen. Our worlds were never going to mix. Please don't make me explain this again; it was hard enough the first time. I'll always care for you, but we have to say goodbye now.

"I'm fine." Ha! The biggest lie she'd ever told. But she wasn't injured or sick or anything, so it would do.

I'm willing to fight for us. Why aren't you?

JK shoved her phone into her pocket once more. She'd been through all this with Tabitha already. Rehashing it wouldn't do either of them any good. She *was* fighting for Tabitha in the best way she knew how, but if Tabitha didn't see it that way, then JK was unlikely to be able to change her mind.

JK didn't respond to the message and Tabitha didn't message again. It was better that way.

JK didn't consider blocking Tabitha. If Tabitha ever really was in trouble—in physical danger—JK wanted to be contactable, just in case Peter's skills weren't up to scratch, which the evidence so far suggested was the case.

She went home after a long day of skulking

outside the mansion and forced herself into the shower before falling onto the couch and turning on the TV. JK didn't really focus on the show she was meant to be watching. Instead, she was thinking of Tabitha, worrying about her.

How long would Tabitha stay in her room, refusing meals? She sounded depressed. Surely, her family would get her professional help if it came to that? The idea that she had caused Tabitha to become ill made JK want to shrivel into a ball and die.

She couldn't stand the thought, but she had to face the fact that it might be true. If it was, there wasn't anything she could do about it except stay far away from Tabitha and give her time and space to heal.

JK would have to be sure not to let Tabitha catch so much as a glimpse of her while she was doing her self-imposed guard duties around the mansion. Soon enough—probably sooner rather than later now that there was nothing holding her here anymore—Tabitha would go back to England and JK would go back to her old life.

The thought was not an appealing one. For now, JK would focus on what she could do— keeping Tabitha safe.

JK skulked around the mansion for another week before there was any movement. She practically jumped for joy when she saw Tabitha *finally* leaving the house... that was, until she really looked at her.

JK only caught a glimpse of Tabitha through the car window at a distance, but she looked pale, drawn and miserable. There were bags under her eyes that belied the fact she had been spending most of her time in bed. She certainly looked like she'd lost weight.

JK reminded herself that it was good Tabitha was leaving the house at all. It had to show that she was moving on.

JK did her usual thing, following from a distance. Unsurprisingly, Tabitha went to a mall. It was one of the ones she and JK had been to together. JK remembered this one—it was the one where Tabitha had seduced her in that lingerie store.

Peter was paying more attention to Tabitha than the people around her, so it was left to JK to survey the crowd and make sure that no one was paying Tabitha too much attention. A few words to Peter from Tabitha convinced him to wait for her outside the lingerie store—a bad move on Peter's part. What if something happened inside the store?

JK pulled her baseball cap down over her eyes and slipped in past Peter and got a glimpse of Tabitha heading to the changing room, though she didn't appear to have any lingerie with her.

JK hurried into an adjacent changing room, pulling the curtain closed to hide herself. The sound of soft crying soon reached her ears. JK realized with a sinking feeling in her stomach that Tabitha was in the exact same cubicle that she had changed in when she'd been trying to seduce JK, which felt like a lifetime ago.

She didn't have anything to try on. It was too soon to make a judgment for sure, but JK suspected she knew what was going on here. Tabitha was coming to places they had both been to together, perhaps to immerse herself in the memories, but those memories were only upsetting her.

JK ached to comfort Tabitha. It was physically painful to sit here and listen to the woman she loved in pain. The only thing that prevented her from acting was the knowledge that if she did, she would cause Tabitha more pain in the long run.

Sure, she could comfort Tabitha now, but it

would be cold comfort, knowing that JK would simply have to leave before Peter caught them and they would need to go their separate ways again.

Not for the first time, she gave brief thought to a secret affair, but she knew it wouldn't work. Tabitha was too closely watched, and if JK followed her to the U.K. there would be a million palace spies watching Tabitha. Sooner or later, someone would find out, and it would all fall apart.

It didn't take long to confirm JK's theory. After the lingerie store, Tabitha went to the movie theater where they had been kicked out for getting intimate in the back row. Then she went to the food court where they eaten burgers together. After that, it was the little nook where they had kissed once.

Watching the pain on Tabitha's face as tears tracked down her beautiful cheeks made JK feel like the world's shittiest person, but there was nothing she could do about that. She wanted to leave—she didn't want to have to watch this—but she couldn't. She had to stay to protect Tabitha. Peter certainly wasn't doing it adequately. He was more interested in spying on Tabitha than actually protecting her.

After several hours of wandering through the mall like a ghost, Tabitha finally went home and didn't emerge for the rest of the day. JK imagined her lying in bed, crying and refusing meals, and had to wipe her own cheeks.

This was the worst feeling in the world. Why the hell did anyone want to fall in love if this was what it felt like?

On her way home, she stopped at the gym and beat up the boxing bag so badly that its leather cover split, sending sand spilling everywhere. After apologizing profusely to the gym owner, JK made a hasty retreat, her frustrations and sorrow far from eased.

When she got home, there was a message waiting on her phone. She winced as she opened it, praying it wouldn't be from Tabitha.

It wasn't. It was from Gray.

Hi, JK. Give me a call when you have a minute.

JK grimaced. She had written a full report for Gray, including the reason she was fired. Gray no doubt wanted to chew her out for her unprofessional behavior, and she would deserve it. Anything would be better than sitting with her current feelings of desolation, even being thoroughly reprimanded by her boss, so she made the call immediately.

"Hi, JK, thanks for getting back to me so quickly."

"Of course." JK waited for the blow to fall.

"How are you doing?"

"What?"

"How are you, JK?"

"Aren't you going to yell at me for sleeping with a client?"

Gray chuckled. "Please, I'm the last one who has any right to get all high and mighty about that. Besides, with the number of my employees who have ended up marrying clients, you'd think we were a matchmaking agency."

Well, this wasn't the way JK had expected the conversation to go. "Uh, thanks, Gray." Why was Gray calling if not to reprimand her? She didn't particularly feel like talking about her feelings, so she decided to change the subject. "How is Savannah doing?"

"Oh, she's great. The first trimester was a bit rough, but everything has settled down nicely.

We're hoping it'll be smooth sailing from here. But that's not why I called. I have another job for you, if you're interested."

JK's heart sank. Of course, that's why Gray would be calling her. She did work for Gray, after all. Now that her work with Tabitha was done, she'd be expected to take on another case.

"I... I can't."

"You're still watching her, aren't you?"

JK couldn't find it in herself to deny it. "Her current bodyguard is doing a great job at spying on her, but actually protecting her? He sucks. He hasn't even noticed I am following them. I'm worried for Tabitha's safety. Her presence here has already been unmasked once."

"I understand. Just make sure you don't get caught following her, JK. That could lead to a lot of trouble on all sides."

"I get it. I don't want to bring bad press to your company. I'll be careful."

"Thanks, JK. Let me know when you're ready to take on another job."

"That'll probably only be when Tabitha leaves," JK admitted.

"I figured as much. Do you have any idea when that'll be?"

"Not really, but I can't see it being that much longer. She's been here a while already, and it hasn't exactly been a positive experience for her. She'll probably want to be heading home sooner rather than later."

"Well, regardless, when you come back to work, I want your full attention, which you can't give me while your heart is still with Tabitha. I'll wait until you're ready."

"Thanks, Gray. Goodnight."

"Goodnight, JK."

Gray had been more understanding than JK deserved. She dreaded the day when Tabitha went back to England—when she would finally have to move on. She gave brief thought to following Tabitha there and watching her from afar, but that was creepy and stalkerish, and she wouldn't do it.

Besides, what kind of life would that be? Watching the woman she loved go about her life, like looking through a pane of one-sided glass, unable to touch or be seen. It would drive JK crazy with longing.

No, JK would wait for Tabitha to leave before trying to pick up the pieces of her life.

Loving Tabitha had forever changed her, and she didn't think she would ever be the same again.

Despite everything, she couldn't bring herself to regret it. Her heart may be broken beyond repair, but she wouldn't exchange the precious time she'd spent with Tabitha for anything. She may live the rest of her life wishing things had been different, but she still had her memories, and no one could take those away from her.

9

TABITHA

"Ma'am, you should eat."

"I'm not hungry, Dan."

"Nevertheless, you still need food."

"You can just leave it here. I'll eat later."

Dan sighed and put down the plate. Tabitha was just drifting off into a blessedly numbing nap when the door opened again.

"Get up."

Her eyes flew open and she propped herself up on an elbow. "*Julie?*"

"Get up, Tabitha. You stink and you look awful. You're taking a shower, and then we're having breakfast together."

"Julie, what are you doing here?" Julie was the

daughter of a high-ranking government official back in England and one of Tabitha's closest friends.

"I got a very worried call from your mother, who has received word that you won't leave your bed and are refusing meals. We're getting you cleaned up and fed, and then we'll talk."

Tabitha groaned and flopped down onto the bed. "I'm tired, Julie. I just want to sleep."

The next thing she knew, the blankets were being ripped away from her. "Julie! Leave me alone!"

"Not a chance. I'm not letting you wallow in whatever you've been stewing in for the past few weeks. We're going to get through this, Tabitha, but you need to work with me here."

"I don't need your help," Tabitha said mulishly.

"Tough shit, because you've got it whether you like it or not. Now get up before I have to resort to more drastic measures."

Tabitha groaned and pulled the pillow over her head, hoping Julie would leave her alone. To her surprise, she heard Julie's footsteps leaving the room. That was easier than she'd thought.

Unfortunately, those footsteps returned a minute later. Tabitha kept the pillow over her head, trying to ignore Julie. Surely, she would give up eventually.

The next thing she knew, freezing water was being poured all over her.

"Fuck!" Tabitha rolled out of bed, away from the jug Julie was pouring from, but it was too late; she was already drenched in ice water. "What the hell, Julie!"

"I've turned the shower on for you. It should be nice and hot by now."

Tabitha glared at Julie, but she was already shivering and a hot shower suddenly sounded good right about now. She grabbed a towel and stalked to the bathroom.

Once she was in the warm water, she decided she may as well wash. Surprisingly, she did feel a little better once she was clean, though she wasn't going to admit that to Julie. She trudged back to her room to find that Julie had changed the bed linen and set out a fresh pair of clothes for her.

Tabitha ignored the clothes and reached for her pajamas, but Julie slapped her hands away. "No more sad day pajamas. Get dressed properly."

"You do realize that I'm the future Queen of England, right?"

"And I have orders from the *current* Queen of England, so get dressed."

Tabitha grumbled under her breath as she pulled on the clothes Julie handed her. Once she was dressed, Julie took her by the hand and practically dragged her through to the dining room. The table was already laden with food, and Julie served Tabitha up a big bowl of muesli and fruit salad with yogurt.

"Eat." She leveled Tabitha with a stern gaze.

"I'm not hungry."

"I don't care."

"I'm going to throw up."

"No, you won't. Eat now or I resort to drastic measures."

Not wanting to be drenched in freezing water again, Tabitha reluctantly picked up her spoon. To her surprise, once she started to eat, her appetite started to take notice and she began wolfing down the muesli and fruit salad. She finished the whole bowl, feeling better than she had before.

"Good. Now, we're going for a walk in the garden, and then we'll talk."

"I don't remember you being this bossy," Tabitha muttered.

"I don't remember you being this lacking in

basic self-care, but here we are."

Julie linked her arm with Tabitha's and force-fully guided her outside. Tabitha had to admit that the fresh air was pleasant after nearly a week of not leaving her room. Julie led her to a bench and sat her down.

"Now, tell me what's wrong."

Tabitha sighed. She didn't imagine Julie would let her get out of this, and honestly, she could use someone to talk to. "How much has my mom told you?"

"Not a whole lot. She said that you were caught having an illicit affair with your female bodyguard, who was fired and replaced, and you haven't been yourself ever since. She wanted to get you committed to a very posh rehab centre, but I convinced her to let me try to help first."

Some of Tabitha's resentment melted away. The last thing she needed was to be stuck in some hospital. She'd take Julie and her ice water over that any day.

"Her name is J," Tabitha said softly. "I'm in love with her."

If Julie was surprised by the fact that Tabitha was in love with a woman, she didn't show it. "Tell me more."

So, Tabitha told her. She told Julie about how she and JK got together, and how they had slowly grown closer. She told her about how JK had saved her life, and about Alice's betrayal. Finally, as tears started tracking down her cheeks, she relayed the story of JK's departure.

"She didn't even try to fight for me," Tabitha sobbed. "I love her, and I think she loves me, but she doesn't even care enough to try and find a way for us to be together."

"Oh, Tabitha, I'm so sorry."

Julie pulled Tabitha into a tight hug, letting Tabitha cry on her shoulder. Tabitha wasn't sure how long they stayed like that, but eventually, her tears slowed and she pulled back. "I don't know what to do, Julie. I know I have to move on, but I don't know how. It's like J has taken my heart hostage, and I don't know how to get it back."

"You're looking at this all wrong, Tabitha. From everything you've described, it doesn't sound like J doesn't care for you. She's just scared—scared that being with her will hurt you and you will lose everything. So, she's not willing to fight, not when she fears you may be a casualty in that battle. But *you* can still fight. Every relationship has two sides to it. She may not be fighting for you because she just wants to protect you, but you're not fighting for her, either."

"I don't know how! I've called and texted, but she doesn't want to talk to me, Julie."

"So go to her. *Make* her talk to you. Show her that you're not afraid to incur your mother's wrath. You can't give up on true love, Tabitha. It's too rare and beautiful a thing to be thrown aside."

"Do you really think it'll make a difference?"

"I think that if you don't try, you have no chance whatsoever."

"I'm worried she'll just reject me again. I don't know if my heart can take that."

"Sometimes, you have to take a risk. You might get hurt. But you're hurting now. Honestly, how much worse can it get?"

Julie had a good point there. "Okay. Okay, I'll do it."

"That's my girl. You're a fighter, Tabitha. It's not like you to give up. You were knocked down for a while, but you'll always find your feet again."

Tabitha pulled Julie into another hug. "Thank you, Julie. Only a true friend would stand up for—and to—me like this."

Tabitha still didn't know how many of her friends back home were simply in it for the money, but today had proven one thing for sure. Julie truly cared for her, and Tabitha could count on Julie to be there through good times and bad. That kind of friendship had to be almost as rare as true love, and Tabitha intended to hold onto it.

"I don't know where she lives," Tabitha admitted.

"So call the agency she comes from."

"I doubt they will just give out the addresses of their employees."

"Perhaps not, but it's worth a try. If you don't have any luck there, you can always hire a private investigator."

That seemed sensible. JK couldn't be that hard to find. Tabitha looked up the number for JK's agency and made the call.

"Hello, Gray Reilly speaking."

"Hi, Gray, this is Tabitha. Princess Tabitha."

"Oh... uh... Your Majesty! What can I do for you?"

"I need JK's home address."

"Of course. Do you have a pen handy?"

Tabitha was so surprised that she was momentarily struck speechless. She had expected to have to beg, or at least justify why she wanted to know where JK lived.

"Aren't you going to ask why I want the address of one of your employees?"

"I think I have a fairly good idea. JK... Well, I know she loves you and I know she hasn't been herself lately, to say the least. I think you visiting would be good for her. Rest assured, I don't usually just go handing out the addresses of the people who work for me."

"That's good to know. Thanks, Gray."

Julie handed Tabitha a pen and paper, and Tabitha jotted down the address Gray gave her before thanking her and hanging up.

"Great! I'll see you in a few hours, then."

"Wait, now? I have no idea what to say!"

"Just tell her the truth. You can't do anything more than that."

Tabitha would have liked more time to prepare, but perhaps that was just her making excuses to delay something she was dreading. She wasn't convinced this would go at all well, considering the responses her texts had received so far.

"Alright, I'll go. You'll be here when I get back?" She might need someone to put her back together again.

"Of course. You go get your girl."

Tabitha went to the car and gave Jack the

address. Tabitha was more nervous than she had let on to Julie and half-hoped that they would never get there. However, all too soon, they arrived at JK's house.

Tabitha took a deep breath and marched up to the door. She rang the bell and waited. No answer.

She knocked on the door, but there was no response to that either. Tabitha saw that there was a peephole and wondered if JK was looking through it, seeing her and ignoring her.

"JK, let me in. I'm not leaving until you do. Come on, JK! Like it or not, you're going to talk to me." Tabitha banged on the door, but there was still no response.

Well, she wasn't going to give up that easily. No way was she going back and reporting to Julie that she had left after a mere few minutes. So, she kept knocking and ringing until her fist was sore, but she didn't give up.

"Tab, what are you doing here?"

Tabitha spun around to see JK behind her.

Well, now she felt stupid. JK hadn't been home the whole time. Of course, she couldn't have expected JK to turn into a hermit like she had. JK had probably moved on with her life. "I need to talk to you."

"I'm not sure if that's a good idea."

"Good idea or not, we still need to talk."

JK took a measure of Tabitha's determined expression before sighing and opening the door. "Come in, then."

JK didn't offer her a refreshment, showing her directly to the living room. "What can I do for you, Tabitha?"

Tabitha hated how formal her voice sounded. She remembered how JK's voice usually sounded laden with passion and tenderness and felt a lump rising in her throat as she realized just how badly things had gone between them.

"I have something to say, and I need you to listen. I know you're not willing to fight for us, but you're not the only one in this relationship. I'm here to say that I'm willing to fight for you, J—for us. I'm not going to give up on you, even if you seem to have given up already."

"Tab, we can't—"

"Tell me you don't want me," Tabitha challenged. "Tell me you don't love me, and I swear I'll leave you alone."

JK hesitated. "It's not that simple. There are other factors involved."

"It is that simple, actually. When two people

truly want to be together, when they truly love each other, they face any challenges that life hands them together. Until you tell me that you don't want me, I'm not leaving the U.S. and I'm not moving on. I'll wait for you, J, however long it takes."

"You can't do that, Tab. You know you can't. You have a life to get back to."

"This is my life and I will choose how I want to live it."

JK looked on the verge of tears. "I'm not worth all this, Tab. You're a princess. You can't give up everything for me."

"I will choose what I do and don't want to give up, and you can't stop me. You can control whether you want to be together or not, but you can't control my actions outside of that."

"Tab, please..."

"That's all I have to say. Now, it's your turn, J. Are you willing to try with me? Am I worth fighting for to you?"

JK hesitated for a long moment, leaving Tabitha on tenterhooks, knowing that her entire future would depend on this answer.

"I can't," JK whispered.

Just like that, Tabitha's heart broke.

10

JK

J K watched Tabitha leave, taking yet another piece of her heart with her. The look of devastation on Tabitha's face when JK gave her terrible answer was nearly enough to have JK falling to her knees and begging Tabitha's forgiveness, but she had to remain strong, for Tabitha's sake.

As much as she wanted to dissolve into a puddle on the floor and cry, she couldn't. She still needed to protect Tabitha. So, JK waited a few minutes before following Tabitha back to the mansion. She was becoming quite accomplished at sneaking around the outskirts of the property and avoiding the cameras by now—not that she thought Peter actually put in the effort to check the camera feed regularly.

She watched as Tabitha ran into the arms of her friend, the one who she had cried with earlier today. It made JK's heart ache to see Tabitha in pain and not comfort her, but she was glad that Tabitha at least had a friend there who seemed to be taking up that role.

The friend embraced Tabitha, who was in tears again, then put an arm around her waist and led her inside. It was too risky for JK to get closer to Tabitha's window to see what was going on in her room, but she knew that Tabitha would be safe in the house, at least physically.

Emotionally, it might be a different story. JK worried about how much she had hurt Tabitha, but she worried even more about how she could hurt Tabitha should she give in to what she wanted almost more than anything.

Almost.

Tabitha and her friend didn't emerge from the house for the rest of the day, and JK went home to worry alone. Seeing Tabitha again made her heartsick. She didn't know whether she wished Tabitha hadn't come or not.

On the one hand, it hurt, but on the other, at

least JK had been near her, something she had
thought she would never get to experience again.

She supposed it didn't matter. Tabitha would
never forgive her after this rejection. JK had truly
closed the door on any potential future with her. It
was the right thing to do, but it still hurt so badly
that Tabitha's safety was the only thing stopping JK
from crumpling to the floor and not getting up for
weeks.

She fully expected Tabitha not to leave the
house for at least a week, given her past patterns,
but the very next day, she and her friend—Julie, JK
heard Tabitha calling her—went out for a hike.
Julie was practically dragging a protesting Tabitha
along with her, but Tabitha went anyway, on the
threat of "drastic measures," whatever those were.

JK was just glad that Tabitha had someone
looking out for her. She didn't know if the tough
love approach was the best one in this case, but it
couldn't be good for Tabitha to stay locked up in
the house, stewing in her emotions. Maybe Julie
had the right idea.

JK followed from a distance. She couldn't see
Julie and Tabitha, but she could hear them. Peter
was walking with them, though from what
glimpses she caught of him, he seemed to be

spending more time checking his phone than actually paying attention to their surroundings.

Tabitha and Julie stopped at a clearing, talking about unpacking their picnic lunch. JK crept closer, hiding behind a tree and watching Tabitha. She looked pale and her eyes were puffy, as though she had been crying all night. JK felt like the shittiest person on the planet.

Tabitha and Julie unpacked their lunch and started eating. Julie carried most of the conversation, but Tabitha commented here and there. They offered Peter some food, but before he could accept, his phone started ringing.

"Forgive me, I'll just be a minute."

Then he walked off.

JK stared off at him in indignation. What the hell was he thinking? This was a popular hiking trail! Anyone could come across Tabitha and Julie, and that's not to mention the possibility of someone having followed them here. JK hadn't picked up signs of anyone following, but there were many trails that led parallel to this one and she wouldn't necessarily be able to see an approaching group before they were right upon Tabitha and Julie.

Peter was no doubt taking a call from the

Queen's Chief of Staff. He seemed to deem that more important than Tabitha's safety, and that made JK want nothing more than to punch him in his stupid face.

She took a few steps closer to the tree line, determine to be on hand if anything happened.

The crackling of twigs had her spinning to her left.

Before Tabitha or Julie could react, two men rushed into the clearing. One of them grabbed Tabitha and started dragging her away. The other one pushed Julie away aggressively as if warning her not to come any closer. JK could here the engine of a vehicle from behind the treeline.

It might be too fast for Tabitha and Julie to react, but it wasn't too fast for JK.

JK moved fast and with her unarmed combat skills quickly grabbing and twisting the arm of Tabitha's captor until he screamed in pain and let go of Tabitha.

JK reached into her backpack. She had a Stun Gun in there which would disable these men long enough that she could tie them up and then get the police there to deal with them. She moved swiftly and fired two shots taking both men to the ground.

She followed up quickly by taking cable ties from her bag and binding their wrists and ankles while they were incapacitated.

Tabitha's and Julie's screams trailed off as they realized what had happened.

"J?" Tabitha whispered, tears on her cheeks, her eyes flicking from the downed men to JK's face.

"I'm here, Tab. It's okay."

Tabitha flew toward her and flung herself into JK's arms. JK was there to catch her, embracing her fiercely. "I love you," JK murmured into Tabitha's hair. Her hair smelled of the tropical flowers of her favorite shampoo and JK just wanted to lose herself in it forever.

Seeing Tabitha at so much risk made everything shockingly clear.

JK had been a fool. Tabitha was willing to fight for them. JK was a coward, not wanting to face the difficulties that would come with pursuing their relationship. Those difficulties would fall mostly on Tabitha, but if Tabitha said she could handle it, then that was her choice.

In the end, was JK really any better than these men, trying to take Tabitha's choices away from her? She had been so busy trying to avoid feeling guilty for Tabitha losing her lifestyle that she'd failed to see what was really important.

"I love you too, J," Tabitha sobbed.

"I'm so sorry I hurt you. I love you so much. I made an awful, awful mistake. I can't leave you, Tab. I can't bear to be away from you for a second. I want to fight for us, Tab, if you'll give me a chance."

Tabitha pulled back to look at her, so beautiful even when she was in tears. "You hurt me, J. I thought I could trust you, trust our love, and you crushed my heart."

"I know, sweetheart. I can never truly make up for it, but if you let me, I want to spend the rest of my life trying. Please, will you forgive me?" JK felt her own tears flooding down her face.

Tabitha leaned in and pressed a soft kiss to JK's lips. "I would forgive you anything, J. I love you so much. I know you were only trying to protect me. I know this isn't going to be easy, but we can face it together."

"Together," JK agreed, pulling Tabitha back into her arms.

A moment later, Peter hurtled into the clearing. "What happened?" he demanded, staring at the bound men on the ground.

JK let go of Tabitha and stalked toward

Peter. "I'll tell you what happened. While you were off on your phone call, I disabled these kidnappers. If it was down to you, Tab would be taken by now. I think I can speak for both Tabitha and the Queen when I say that you're fired!"

Peter paled but didn't bother to try to defend himself. He knew that his actions were unforgiveable and nothing was going to save his job at this point.

"I'm taking Tab and Julie home. I suggest you call the police and see that these guys are taken into custody. It's the least you can do."

Peter nodded dismally. "I'll see to it that it's done."

"Good. Tab, Julie. Come. We're going home."

Tabitha and JK held hands the whole way back down the hiking trail. Both she and Julie were jumpy and kept turning to look at things JK couldn't see or hear.

"It's okay," she said steadily. "The threat has been neutralized for now. We'll be back at the car soon, and I'll get you home."

"Thank you for saving us," Julie said in a small voice. "How did you even find us?"

"I've been following Tab," JK admitted. "Peter

was doing a shit job of looking after her, and I wasn't going to leave her unprotected."

"You saved our lives—our hero!" Tabitha gave JK an adoring look that JK was sure was mirrored on her own face.

They made it to the car without incident and Jack wasted no time in getting them home. He didn't question JK's presence or Peter's absence. JK supposed that as a driver, he must have gotten used to transporting clients without getting involved in their personal business.

When they got home, Tabitha and Julie hugged shakily. "Julie, can you call my mom? Tell her I need her here, in the U.S. The two of us need to talk."

"Of course. One way or another, she'll be here."

"I know. You're more resourceful than I ever gave you credit for and I'm lucky to have you as a friend."

"I'm just glad everything has worked out— well, almost. You still need to sort things out with your mother, but I don't think it'll go as badly as you're imagining. She may be set in her ways, but I think she loves you more than she loves tradition."

"I guess we'll see, won't we?" Tabitha murmured. She turned to JK. "Take me to bed?"

"Your wish is my command, Princess." JK smiled.

JK swept Tabitha off her feet and carried her through to the bedroom. Tabitha giggled the whole way and wriggled to be put down once they were inside, but JK didn't let go, kicking the door closed and carrying Tabitha all the way to the bed.

"I just want to hold you. Is that ok? We have all the time in the world for everything else." JK kissed Tabitha for a moment before pulling back to speak. "I have a lot to make up for. I want to show you exactly how much I love you. Will you let me, Tab?"

"Always, J."

JK grinned and held her close, inhaling the scent of her as though it was the first time. She knew she never ever wanted to let go. She was the luckiest woman in the world.

The next few weeks were likely to be insane. If Tabitha was indeed disowned, she and JK would need to scramble to pull their lives together. JK had enough savings to support them for now, but god knows what Tabitha's life would be like if she suddenly had no money but still had all the fame and the issues that came with being who she was.

It was terrifying, but they would have to find a way to face things together.

JK didn't fool herself that it was going to be easy, and it was likely that neither of them would have the time nor the inclination to be intimate in the near future. She wanted to take advantage of this time now, to give them both a sweet memory to hold onto when things got hard.

One thing, she was sure of. This wasn't going to be easy, but it was going to be worth it.

JK kissed Tabitha again, claiming Tabitha's mouth with her tongue. Tabitha melted into the kiss, returning it sweetly, her tongue twining divinely with JK's.

JK pulled Tabitha's shirt off and reached down with one hand to start twisting Tabitha's nipples gently, first one and then the other.

"J, spank me," Tabitha gasped.

It wasn't what JK was expecting, but it certainly wasn't unwelcome. "Turn over, then."

"No, here." Tabitha pulled JK's wrist back to her breasts.

"Ooh, someone is becoming kinky."

"Shut up," Tabitha mumbled.

JK chuckled and brought her flat hand down sharply on Tabitha's breast, right over the nipple.

Tabitha gasped and tensed, causing JK to pause. "Is that okay?"

"Yes!" Tabitha had a naughty gleam in her eye.

So, JK slapped her breasts again, and again, not too hard- she didn't want to do any damage- until Tabitha was moaning and writhing beneath her. Tabitha reached down to push her hand inside her own jeans but JK wasn't having any of that.

"No, no, what I'd really like today is you to sit on my face."

JK rolled onto her back and motioned Tabitha forward. Tabitha moaned and flipped a leg over JK's head, positioning her clit right above JK's mouth. JK could already feel her chin becoming slick with Tabitha's juices and she loved it.

Tabitha immediately started rocking against JK, whimpering as JK licked her clit steadily, working her up into a frenzy.

Tabitha's moans grew loud and intense and JK knew she was close.

JK loved that it had barely been a minute and she already had Tabitha on the edge. She wondered how long it had been since Tabitha had come. She certainly hadn't felt masturbating in the time since she and Tabitha had been apart and could only imagine that Tabitha felt the same way.

JK grabbed Tabitha's round ass and squeezed. Tabitha screamed as she came, convulsing on JK's tongue. JK lapped it every bit of her wetness, enjoying every moment of it. Tabitha tasted delicious, and JK wouldn't complain if she got to do this every day for the rest of her life.

Tabitha went limp, just managing to fall to the side rather than squash JK. Fortunately, the bed was big enough to accommodate her. Her leg ended up awkwardly draped across JK's neck, but Tabitha seemed perfectly comfortable.

"That was amazing. *You're* amazing, J. I missed you so much."

"Let's just say that I have plenty of inspiration." JK was already touching herself, nearly as desperate to come as Tabitha had been.

"Hey, don't do that. I want to make you come, too. Just give me a minute."

"I can't," JK panted. "I need to come now, Tabitha."

Tabitha gave her a wicked grin. "Fine, keep touching yourself... but don't come until I can see to you."

"Turning the tables on me, are you?"

"Do you like it?"

"Fuck, yes." JK could already feel her orgasm

building and brought herself right to the edge before easing off, not stopping but barely touching herself except for feather-light brushes against her clit. Soon, even those became too much and she had to remove her hand completely lest she come before it was time.

She didn't last long; her hand being drawn back to her clit almost magnetically after less than half a minute. JK moaned as sparks of divine pleasure tingled through her body. She was so close and needed to come so badly...

Tabitha's breathing had evened out and she was watching JK through heavily lidded eyes. JK was sure she was recovered by now, but she continued to watch, to tease JK with her gaze.

"Tab, fuck, I need you. Please, get me off."

It was as though Tabitha had been waiting for her to ask.

"Lie back."

JK practically threw herself back on the bed and spread her legs. Tabitha wasted no time in crawling between them and bringing her mouth to JK's clit.

JK wanted to enjoy the feeling of Tabitha's tongue, but her body had other ideas. A mere two licks and she was coming hard, her pussy clenching as she released onto the bed beneath her.

Tabitha chuckled as she sat up. "We should do that more often."

"I certainly won't be complaining. I see why you like it so much."

The two of them settled into each other's arms. JK was finding it difficult to be upset about the kidnapping attempt on Tabitha. Of course, she regretted the fact that Tabitha had been through such a trauma, but it had brought them together, and JK was so grateful for that fact that she could muster very little resentment for the entire incident.

JK didn't know what the next day would bring, but she knew that she and Tabitha would face it together, and for now, that was enough.

11

TABITHA

The next morning, Tabitha and JK were woken early by a knock on the door.

"What?" Tabitha moaned. She and JK had been up late making love and she was in no mood to be forced to breakfast under threat of being drenched in cold water.

"Tab, J, it's Julie. You need to get up now."

"Go away," JK moaned, pulling the blanket further up on both of them.

"She'll pour water on us," Tabitha warned.

"I'll protect you."

Tabitha was satisfied with that and was just settling down to drift off again when the door opened. "You had better both be decent, because I'm coming in."

JK moved herself into a sitting position between Tabitha and Julie. "If I see you with a jug of water, Julie, I'm taking you down."

Julie chuckled as she stepped inside, with no jug in sight. "Good to see your protective instincts are fully functional. No, I don't think that'll be necessary today. I just came to tell you that your mother's flight lands in an hour, Tab. You should probably get dressed and ready to receive her."

That certainly woke Tabitha up. The rush of adrenaline had her sitting bolt upright. "An hour? What in the world did you say to get her here so fast?"

Julie raised an eyebrow. "Does it matter?"

"On second thought, no. I actually don't want to know. Thanks, Julie. We'll be down for breakfast in a bit."

When Julie left, Tabitha headed toward the shower. "I'll join you," JK offered. "Not for sexy times," she said in response to Tabitha's raised eyebrow. "I wish, but we don't have time for that. Let's just wash each other and get dressed."

Their hands may have lingered on each other's skin for slightly longer than necessary, but they got out of the shower in good time. Tabitha got dressed on one of her smarter outfits- very different to how she had been dressing the past few weeks, and did her hair and make up immaculately and advised JK on what to wear for her first meeting with the queen.

The two of them had a quick breakfast with Julie before going to the lounge to wait. They hadn't been waiting long before the doorbell rang.

Tabitha took a deep breath and went to the door. There was her mother, two members of her British Police Protection Team standing behind her.

"Mom, thank you for coming."

"Tabitha, what is going on? Are you okay?"

"Please, come inside. We have a lot to talk about today." Tabitha didn't know exactly what Julie had told her mother, but she looked extremely worried, which just went to show, as if it hadn't been adequately demonstrated already, that Julie would choose to have Tabitha's back when it really counted, even if it meant risking the wrath of the Queen of England herself.

Her mother followed her inside but stopped short at the sight of JK. "Are you the bodyguard? What are you doing here?" she snapped.

"Don't talk to JK like that! This is my house, and you will show my guests respect."

"Your house? You forget that *I'm* the one paying for this place, Tabitha."

"Actually, no," Tabitha said calmly. "I spoke to the owner. I bought this house last week."

JK covered her mouth with her hand as she coughed, which did a fairly good job of hiding her chuckle.

Mary's nostrils flared, but she didn't argue. "Very well. Let's talk, Tabitha. JK, you may wait out in the hall. By Peter's absence, I presume you have re-hired JK as your bodyguard?"

"Actually, no. That's part of what I need to talk to you about, and J is going to be part of that conversation."

Her mother frowned but nodded. "Very well. Lead the way, Tabitha."

JK sat down next to Tabitha on the couch, while her mother sat opposite them. Her bodyguards stood behind her, their eyes darting around the room.

"Give us the room," she nodded to them.

"Well? What is going on, Tabitha?"

Tabitha took a deep breath, trying to quell her nerves. JK took her hand and squeezed.

"Mom, I'm gay."

"Well, yes, I had assumed as much—or at least

something along those lines. You've never been interested in men. Why do you think I've never pushed you for marriage?"

"You're... You're okay with it?"

Mary's expression softened. "Of course I am, Tabitha. I'm sorry if I ever gave you the impression that I would condemn you for your sexuality. It is just... well... obviously complicated by who you are, but we can get to that bit. We will find a way. I just wish you'd told me sooner."

Well, so far, so good.

"I'm in love with JK."

The understanding expression vanished at once. "This is where the difficulty arises."

"Difficulty or not, that is the case, and I'm not going to pretend otherwise anymore. I'm going to be with JK, whether it is difficult or not."

Mary's eyes narrowed. "I don't think you understand, Tabitha. I have the power to ruin you, if I choose. You would do best not to cross me."

JK spoke up. "The only thing you have the power to do is disown her. You think she would be alone in the world if you did that, but she wouldn't. She'd have me. Tabitha is far from helpless. It may take some time, but I have utter confidence that she would find a way to flourish in the world without you. I can support her until she finds her feet. She'll be just fine without you. I have her back."

"As do I." Tabitha hadn't even noticed Julie coming in, but she stepped forward now, glaring at Mary. "Tabitha is my best friend, and I am fully prepared to take her and JK in, or support them financially from afar if they choose to stay in the U.S. You don't have as much control over your daughter as you think you do."

Mary looked positively apoplectic. "You—you would abandon your duty?"

"Mom, I don't want to abandon anything. I have every intention of being Queen one day and fulfilling my duties to England, but I'm not willing to sacrifice my happiness to do that, nor do I think it's fair of you to ask me to. Do you really want me to live a life of misery just because you think the woman I love doesn't hold a high enough station to be politically appropriate?"

"You would get over her. You could find someone so much better."

"No, she wouldn't!" Julie snapped. "You didn't see her when I arrived. She was a mess. You yourself wondered if we'd have to admit her."

"Depression is temporary."

"A broken heart isn't! You should know that, Mom!"

Mary flinched but didn't protest. Tabitha knew it was a low blow, bringing her father up, but it was the only way she could think to bring her point across. Mary had never recovered from his death, and she carried the pain with her every day.

"That's different," Mary whispered.

"It's not. J is the love of my life. Either you accept that and find a way to help us, or I will walk away from the British monarchy. I choose her, Mom. I love you and I do want to fulfil my responsibility as your heir, but if it comes down to a choice, I'm choosing J over everything. She makes me happier than I have ever been. Happier than I could ever have imagined was possible."

Mary was silent for a long time, considering her daughter. Eventually, her eyes moved to JK. "What do you have to say about this, JK?"

"Your Majesty, I love your daughter more than anything in the world. I would move heaven and Earth to make her happy and I fully intend to give her everything she deserves, as much as I am able to. I am so unbelievably lucky to have found her, and as long as she wants to be with me, I am not letting her go for anything. I know this is not easy.

Believe me, I know we come from different worlds. But, I can learn. I can be who you need me to be to fit into the monarchy."

Silence once more fell over the room. Tabitha wondered if she should say something else to strengthen her case but decided that she had said enough. It would be better to give Mary some time to digest it all.

After a few agonizing minutes, Mary sighed, some of the tension going out of her shoulders. "Tabitha, I grew up with a lot of expectations placed on me, and I passed those expectations on to you. Perhaps they are outdated now. I want things to work out well politically, but more than that, I want you to be happy. This isn't easy for me to accept, but if JK is truly who you need... Well, then I will support you. We will take advice on how best to bring her into the family."

Tabitha played the words over several times in her head, unable to believe what she'd just heard. "Y-you'll accept JK?"

"You'll still need to get married, and I expect heirs, but yes, I will publicly and personally support your relationship."

"You don't have to worry there, Your Majesty. I have every intention of marrying your daughter and raising a family with her, should that be what she wants, too."

Tabitha turned to face JK, tears pricking in the corners of her eyes. "Really?" she whispered.

"Really. Don't worry, I'll do a proper proposal when the time is right. I'm sure it'll need to be a big event with the press and the right people around."

Mary gave JK the first genuine smile Tabitha had seen directed at her. "You know, I think you're going to fit in around here just fine, JK. Please, call me Mary. I'm to be your mother-in-law, after all."

"Thank you, Mary." JK stood and the two of them moved into an awkward embrace. It didn't matter. There was time for the awkwardness to thaw, for them to become more comfortable with each other. What was important was that they were both willing to try.

"You know what this means, right, J? Are you really willing to move to England? To sit by my side in many years time when I become Queen and rule alongside me?"

"For you, Tab, anything. It's not at all where I saw my life going, but that's just because I never envisioned anyone as perfect as you coming into my life. I'm sure it'll take a lot of getting used to, and I have a lot of learning to do, but we can handle it, together."

"I'll be with you through all of it, just like you were with me through this—just like you would have been with me should this conversation have gone the other way."

"As will I. I know all the ins and outs that members of the royal family might not. I've got your back too, J." Julie said to them both.

"Thanks, Julie. And thank you for being such a true friend to Tabitha. I know she couldn't ask for anyone better supporting her."

"I should get going, since our business is concluded."

"You don't need to rush out, Mom. At least stay for the day. We can have lunch and dinner together—you and J can get to know each other a bit better. I'm sure you'll be fast friends once you get past the initial stages of introduction."

"OK," Mary smiled. "I'd love to spend the day with you both. Although I think if we go out, my presence will draw some attention. How will you cope with the press when you are back in the UK, Tabitha?"

"I don't think that'll be a problem anymore." Tabitha gave her mother a small smile. "I think part of the reason I didn't want the media shining a light on my life was because of how lonely and alone I felt a lot of the time. It just highlighted my own unhappiness to me, and I hated it. Now, my heart is full, and seeing my joy spread across the pages of newspapers and magazines... Well, I can't imagine it'll bother me."

JK's shoulders relaxed a little. "As long as you're happy, I'm happy."

She put an arm around Tabitha and Tabitha leaned her head on JK's shoulder. Mary smiled.

Everything was going to be okay.

EPILOGUE

"I don't get it. It's just a fork. Why is it so important?"

"Honestly, it's not," Tabitha admitted. "Everyone thinks it is, but really, in the grand scheme of things, who really cares what utensils you use? However, my mom wants you to learn the proper protocol, and I think we should at least put in some token effort."

"Agreed," JK sighed. "Show me the difference again."

The utensils lesson ended up with them doing a mini duel with their forks as swords, which drew scandalized looks from some of the staff, but Tabitha didn't care. She and JK were having fun, and that was all that really mattered.

"It's time for your pills."

"Oh yes! Really, I don't know what I would do without you." Tabitha pulled JK in for a brief kiss before taking the box JK handed her and downing a few pills. She was on a fertility treatment, getting ready for artificial insemination. They had already picked out the perfect sperm donor- a top diplomat and good friend of Tabitha's mother's son who Tabitha had always liked- although all of this was very top secret from public knowledge- and would be going in for the procedure in less than a month.

Though they had only been married for six months now, they were both more than ready to start a family. Mary was delighted that she would hopefully soon have a grandchild.

As Tabitha had expected, once the initial awkwardness faded, she and JK had quickly become close, bonded by their love for Tabitha.

"Do you think we'll get any protesters at the clinic?" Tabitha asked.

"I think if we do, they'll be out-shouted by our supporters."

That was true enough. They had always had far more support than they'd had hate. Tabitha remembered her coming out, just under two years ago now.

"I can't look! J, look for me."

"Give it here, sweetheart. Don't worry, I'm sure it'll be fine." JK took Tabitha's phone and glanced at Twitter. Already, tweets were coming in by the dozens.

Just half an hour ago, Tabitha had done the interview of a lifetime, where she not only came out as gay, but also announced her relationship with JK to the rest of the world. They had been planning this for months now, going over speeches and possible questions the interviewer could ask.

In public, JK had been acting as Tabitha's bodyguard. Both she and Tabitha were more than ready to be able to kiss and hold hands outside of the privacy of their now soundproofed bedroom.

"It's good, love! I mean, there are a few homophobes, like we expected, but, let's see—maybe nine out of ten of them are positive. They're calling you an inspiration to lesbians worldwide. Oh! Look, there are other women coming out in response right now and tagging you. Some of them are as young as twelve and thirteen. Tab, this is wonderful."

Tabitha felt tears threatening and took a deep breath. "I'm sure the hate will come."

"It will," JK agreed. "When it does, though, we will face it head-on. Try to take the win, love. You've gained the adoration of many." She glanced at the phone again. "People are praising your decision to be with someone not of noble birth. They say you're breaking a cycle that never should have been there to begin with."

"What about other royalty around the world?"

JK scrolled for a few minutes before responding. "Surprisingly positive. There's one family here that's spewing hate, but I count at least three others who are openly supportive. One prince is saying that his best friend is gay and he's glad that the queer community is getting some representation among royalty."

It was all too much. The tears spilled over, but they were tears of joy and relief. "I can't believe it. We actually did it."

"You did it. I was just there to support."

"Please. Like I wouldn't have run for the hills before they could ask the first question if you hadn't been there giving me a thumbs up behind the camera."

"I'll always be there for you, Tab. No matter what."

. . .

Tabitha looked at her list. "We still need to go over the protocol for how to deal with foreign royalty."

"Yeah? I bet I can convince you to postpone that lesson." JK pressed a kiss to Tabitha's earlobe.

"We shouldn't. It's our duty."

"It's my primary duty to love you. Once you're pregnant, you never know how you'll feel. You may be fine, but you may feel gross and not want to have sex at all. We should take advantage of this time while we have it."

That was a difficult argument to refute. "Well, I suppose it can't hurt to delay a little..."

JK captured Tabitha's lips in a kiss. Tabitha kissed her back, ignoring the disapproving sniff from one of the staff members who was passing through the dining room. She wasn't going to stop kissing her wife in her own home just because some people were stuffy and didn't approve of public displays of affection.

JK lifted Tabitha up and Tabitha wrapped her legs easily around JK's waist. JK was well acquainted with the palace gym and regularly worked out, leaving her easily able to heft Tabitha's weight, something that never failed to turn Tabitha on.

Tabitha ignored the titters as JK carried her

through to their bedroom and laid her down on the bed.

"I want you bound and helpless before me," JK growled in Tabitha's ear.

A shiver of desire went through Tabitha's body. "Yes, please."

There were leather ties attached under the bead that the housekeepers had long ago stopped raising their eyebrows at. Tabitha wriggled out of her clothes and spread herself out on the bed, arms and ankles near the edges. JK tied her up and started kissing her, working from her left ankle up to her upper thigh before skipping over her pussy and going to her right ankle and working her way up again.

"J..." Tabitha complained as JK once more bypassed her pussy to start pressing wet kisses to her stomach.

"No complaining, or I'm going to gag you."

Hm, that sounded fun. Maybe Tabitha should complain some more... but then JK took one of Tabitha's nipples into her mouth, and Tabitha forgot all about that train of thought.

JK sucked on her nipple, so lightly that Tabitha could barely feel her there, but when Tabitha moaned urgently and shifted beneath her, as much as the ropes would allow, JK rewarded her with a firmer pressure.

She could feel her pussy soaking the bed beneath her, but they had long ago put waterproof sheets under their normal sheet.

Tabitha let her eyes slip closed, enjoying the sensations, and therefore didn't see when JK reached a hand between her legs. She got a brief warning when JK used her fingers to reach between Tabitha's folds before she was having her clit rubbed.

"Ahh... yes please, J, just there! Ugh, that's so good!"

Tabitha tried to squirm, but the cuffs prevented it. The feeling of being at JK's mercy was such a turn on that she knew it wouldn't last long if JK kept touching her clit like that.

JK's fingers suddenly disappeared, and Tabitha whined in protest, but JK wasn't gone for long. The next thing Tabitha knew, JK was pressing a big dildo into her with one hand while going back to rubbing her clit with the other. Tabitha tilted her hips into the motion, moaning wantonly as she took everything JK gave her.

"I'm close," she panted, wondering if JK was going to tease her by pulling back and denying her, but it seemed that JK was impatient today, because she doubled down, thrusting and rubbing even faster, driving Tabitha over the edge like a car careening off a cliff.

The binds creaked as Tabitha's whole body arched up, pulling against them, the pleasure roaring through every nerve ending she had.

When it finally ended, she lay lax and panting, trying to get her breath back.

JK didn't give her much time to recover. "I want your tongue. Are you ready for me?"

She was still out of breath and a little light-headed from her orgasm, but JK sounded truly desperate, and Tabitha wasn't going to deny her. "I'm ready for you."

JK swung a leg over Tabitha's head, spreading herself open and pressing her clit against Tabitha's mouth.

Tabitha let her tongue flick out, teasing JK with a light touch. JK moaned and rocked her hips forward, mashing her clit right up against Tabitha's face.

Tabitha loved the feeling of JK taking her pleasure from her while she lay tied up and helpless. If she hadn't just had such an amazing orgasm, she would be squirming with need at the sight. As it was, she was sure that her body wasn't going to take long to wake up and pay attention.

In the end, her body didn't have time to wake up and pay attention. JK braced her hands on the headboard and rocked herself steadily into Tabitha's tongue. She couldn't have lasted more than a minute before she was coming, slicking Tabitha's face and the bed on either side of her with her release.

JK leaned heavily against the headboard for several seconds before forcing herself up to untie Tabitha. As soon as the binds were undone, Tabitha crawled easily into JK's arms. It was her favorite place to be and many times, she had spent the entire day here in bed with her wife, sometimes having sex, but sometimes just cuddling and being close to each other.

"Are you still up for heading out to the beach later?"

Tabitha nodded. "Yeah, definitely—though we'll have to shower first. We're kind of sticky."

"Agreed. There might be press taking photos."

Tabitha shrugged. "Best get some good photos in before I become a whale."

"You'll be the sexiest whale ever to grace the land."

Tabitha had to chuckle at that. It had taken her some time, but with JK's help, she had finally gotten over her aversion to reporters. It helped to know that she was being photographed next to the woman she loved, and that every photo taken could be looked back on to remember their wonderful life together.

After a quick shower, they made their way out to the beach where they smiled for the cameras and said smiled and spoke to anyone who approached them. It was a beautiful day for a walk on the beach, but they cut it short to return to their favorite place. Their home.

They spent the evening in bed. Tabitha drilled JK on some of the things she'd taught her about the various protocols for royalty. A lot of things were expected of her already, and she had risen to those expectations spectacularly, but when Tabitha became Queen, those expectations would rise exponentially.

"Of course, you know the main thing that will change when you become Queen?"

"What's that?"

"My duty and purpose in life right now to love and guard my princess. Then, it'll be to love and guard my Queen."

"I couldn't ask for a better protector—or a better wife. I love you, J. So much."

"I love you, too, Tab. You are the light of my life, and you always will be."

They declined going down to dinner that night, taking it up in their room, eating in bed and watching Netflix, talking late into the night.

Tabitha knew that things would change when the baby came along, but she was ready to face that change head-on with JK. JK would be an amazing mom and Tabitha would be privileged to raise a child with her.

For so long, she had thought that she would live a life of misery, forced to marry a man and live in lovelessness and denial. Some days, she still couldn't believe how perfectly everything had come together.

"Do you ever miss it?" Tabitha murmured. "Your life in America?"

"Not for a second," JK said without hesitation. "I'm right where I need to be, here with you, and soon enough, with our child."

Tabitha couldn't agree more.

ALSO BY EMILY HAYES

If you enjoyed this one, I think you will love the next
book in the Bodyguard Series, check it out below!

**Her job was as a bodyguard, but it quickly became
clear that protecting the client wasn't her only duty...**

*This is an Age Gap, Ice Queen, Butch-Femme
Bodyguard/Actress Romance. Super steamy and always a
Happy Ever After.*

Experienced bodyguard Romy Russell is tasked with protecting Emerald Crowle- a famous Hollywood actress and screen legend. She is 58 years old and very wealthy and powerful. Emerald is in the middle of messy divorce from 3rd husband who has been threatening her.

Emerald is a frosty and demanding Ice Queen who is very used to getting what she wants. It isn't long before the beautiful and seductive Emerald's demands on her bodyguard become sexual. Will Romy give in to them? And if she does, what will happen next?

mybook.to/Bodyguard5

VIP READERS LIST

Hey! Thank you so much for reading my book. I am honestly so very grateful to you for your support. I really hope you enjoyed it.

If you enjoyed it, I would love you to join my VIP readers list and be the first to know about freebies, new releases, price drops and special free *hot* short stories featuring the characters from my books.

You can get a FREE copy of Her Boss by joining my VIP readers list : https://BookHip.com/MNVVPBP

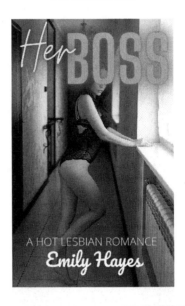

Meg has had a crush on her hot older boss the whole time she has worked for her. Could it be that the fantasies aren't just in Meg's head? https://BookHip.com/MNVVPBP